Berli

Sex, m any of Nick Carter's assignments, and when he was ordered to Germany he found them all.

Sex meant Helga, the beautiful nude Nick fished out of the Rhine more dead than alive.

Money, billions of dollars, fuelled the activities of the neo-Nazis. But whose money . . . who was spending a fortune to help another Fuehrer grab power in Germany?

Death ended the career of two top U.S. agents on the case. And it followed Nick relentlessly from the minute he arrived—from the grimy back alleys of East Berlin to a stinking dungeon hidden somewhere in West Germany.

Berlin

Nick Carter

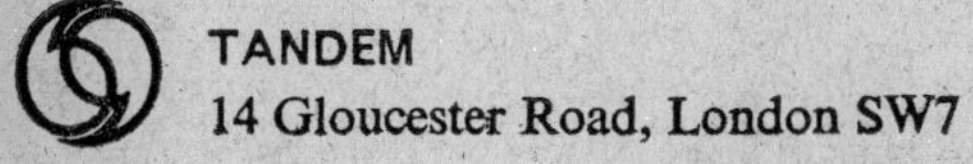
TANDEM
14 Gloucester Road, London SW7

Originally published in the United States by Universal Publishing & Distributing Corporation, 1969
Published in Great Britain by Universal-Tandem Publishing Co. Ltd, 1969

Reprinted 1971

 Produced by Lyle Kenyon Engel

Dedicated to
The Men of the Secret Services
of the
United States of America

Made and printed in Great Britain by
Hunt Barnard Printing Ltd., Aylesbury, Bucks.

I

Waiting is something I've never been particularly good at. They say that's a characteristic of people who are essentially action people. I guess that's me then. Oh, I've sat for hours on hours waiting for a Chinese Communist agent to show himself or to get my hands on a particular sadist. But that's a different kind of waiting. I'm not sure it's waiting, at all, but only a quiet form of action. But the kind of waiting I was doing now, just sitting, was definitely not for me.

The middle Rhineland is unquestionably a lovely, lush, verdant country. The hillsides are green. Alpine flowers of violet, rose and gold roll down the mountainsides to the very edge of the river. The road is winding, interesting at every turn. Little storybook farms and wide-beamed houses pop up unexpectedly. The huge castles that line both banks, the great *Schlosses* of the medieval Teutonic knights, are truly *wunderbar*, magnificent and striking. The *mädchens* are maddeningly friendly and full-bodied, almost eager. Most of them show the result of a little too much "würst" to be my ideal, but I found myself wishing for time to investigate the scene properly.

Maybe it's because it is all so very opulent and breathtaking, but it's even more of a pain when you're in a sweat to catch a boat and your damned rented Opel breaks down. You want to look at it all, you want to enjoy it all, you want to revel in it, but you can't. All you can do is wait and grow impatient and feel frustrated and think of how much worse you'll feel when the Chief learns you didn't show.

My German is more than fair, and I'd flagged a passing motorist and asked him to send some help. From where my rented chariot had broken down I could see the Rhine below and looking north the roofs and church spire of Marksburg. Beyond, just out of range, was Koblenz where I was to meet the Rhine excursion boat, the popular *Ausflugschiffe*. As there was absolutely nothing to do but wait, I opened the car door, let in some air and thought back to the fun I was having in Lucerne only this morning.

After my relatively small part in the Martinique-Montreal affair, I'd gone up to Switzerland to see Charley Treadwell and the ski-and-sun chalet he owned just outside Lucerne itself. It was a grand and proper reunion of old friends, full of boozing and reminiscing. It was Charley who introduced me to Anne-Marie. French and Swiss, with a little Kraut tossed in for leavening, Anne-Marie was pert and fun to be with. Medium height with short, cropped hair and dancing brown eyes, she was a terror on the ski runs and a dream in bed. We tried to divide the days up evenly.

Of course, like every AXE agent, I had to call headquarters and let Hawk know where I could be reached. It was a part of the AXE instant-action network that allowed Hawk to put his finger on a man at all times and all places. It was also a sure-fire way to louse up a good time, I'd found out long ago. I found it out again in Lucerne with Anne-Marie. It was six o'clock in the morning when the phone in my room jangled and I heard Hawk's flat, dry voice. Anne-Marie's lovely arm was casually tossed across my chest, her breasts a soft blanket pressing into me.

"This is the Amalgamated Press and Wire Services," Hawk's voice said crisply. It was a wide-open line, of course, and he was using the usual cover. "Is that you, Nick?"

"It's me," I said. "I'm just thrilled at hearing from you."

"You're not alone," he said at once. The old fox knew me like the proverbial book. Too well, I often thought. "How close is she?" he asked.

"Pretty close."

I could see his gray eyes, steely behind the rimless spectacles, trying to build a quick picture of how close was close.

"Close enough to hear?" came the next question.

"Yes, but she's asleep."

"We don't want to be scooped on this story," Hawk went on, deciding to continue to play it cozy. "One of our photographers, Ted Dennison, has something really big. I believe you worked with Ted on a story once, didn't you?"

"Yes, I know him," I answered. Ted Dennison was one of the best AXE men in the European theater and years ago we had worked on an assignment together. I remembered him as being particularly good at ferreting out information.

"You'll meet Ted aboard the Rhine excursion boat which stops in at Koblenz at three-thirty," Hawk's voice droned. "As he has something really important, if you miss the Rhine excursion steamer at Koblenz, go on to the next stop and board it there. That would be at Mainz at five o'clock."

The phone clicked off and I sighed and slid out from under Anne-Marie. She didn't even stir. That was one of the first things I'd learned about her during our four glorious days together. When she skied, she skied. When she drank, she drank. When she made love, she made love and when she slept, she slept. There were no moderations with this girl. She did everything up to the hilt. I dressed, left her a note saying my boss had called me away and slipped out into the dawn light of Lucerne, cold and still and bracing. I knew that if she had the broken-heart syndrome, which I doubted she'd have, Charley

Treadwell would pat her head and hold her hand. I caught a plane to Frankfurt and the glorious Rhine.

And so I was here, treading the same ground where Caesar, Attila, Charlemagne, Napoleon and all the modern-day conquerors had marched their legions, sitting in a broken-down, rented Opel. I tried not to let it all go to my head. I was about to get out and hail another passing motorist when I saw the Volkswagen breakdown van roll up, its small, round winch jutting out from the rear. The young mechanic was round faced, dark haired and polite. He went at the car with Teutonic thoroughness, for which I was grateful, and Teutonic slowness, for which I was somewhat less than grateful. From the cut of my clothes he had quickly seen that I wasn't German and when I told him I was American he made sure to *erklaren* each step as he went along. I finally convinced him my German was pretty good and I could do without his explaining each step. He located the trouble as being in the *vergasser,* the carburetor, and as he was putting in a new one, I watched with gritted teeth as the Rhine excursion boat went past down below.

The boat was out of sight when he finished. I paid him in American money, which brought an especially happy smile to his face, hopped into the little sedan and once more tried to make it believe it was a Ferrari. To its credit, I must say it tried. We took the curving mountain road full out, bouncing along past more charming houses and more forbidding castles, playing dangerously close to that edge where weight and momentum part company.

As the road lowered in a series of swoops and dips, it moved closer to the Rhine and I caught glimpses of the excursion boat up ahead, serenely chugging along. I finally caught up with it precisely at the spot where the road flattened out to run level with the river. I found myself directly opposite the boat and I slowed down. I was going to make it to Koblenz in time. I sighed in relief. I thought of Dennison out there on the boat. At least he was relaxing, enjoying himself in the sun, while I'd spent all day trying to catch up to him. I cast another look at the excursion boat, long and low, with a small cabin amidship and the rest of her open for sightseers to crowd the rails. I was looking across at the boat when it happened, right before my eyes. It was unreal, the damnedest-looking thing I'd ever seen, almost like watching a slow-motion movie. Of course, there were the explosions first, two of them, a smaller one followed by a huge roar as the boilers went up. But it wasn't the explosions which shook me. It was the sight of the cabin section rising up into the air and coming apart. With the cabin, I saw whole sections of the boat start to go off in different directions. Bodies of people arched into the air like Roman candles at a fireworks display.

I braked hard and came to a bouncing, jouncing stop alongside the riverbank. It was still raining debris over the river as I got out of the Opel, and the excursion boat had all but disappeared. Only the bow and stern sections remained and were falling in on each other. The spot in the river looked as thought some giant hand had suddenly dumped a load of driftwood and debris there. I was struck by the strange silence over everything, following the initial explosions. There were a few cries, the soft hiss of steam meeting water, but largely there was silence. I stripped off everything but my shorts, putting Wilhelmina, my Luger, and Hugo, the pencil-thin stiletto strapped to my forearm, under my clothes. I dived into the Rhine and struck out for the scene. There'd be damned few people alive, I knew, but there was always the chance there might be someone left to save. I knew that calls to the police and to hospitals would have already started from the houses lining the river and on ahead I saw a small tug turning around in mid-river to steam back.

Sections of wood floated past me, torn, jagged, splintered pieces of hull, rail and timbers. Bodies, some equally torn and jagged, drifted by. It was then I saw an arm slowly rise out of the water, trying to swim. I moved toward the blond head attached to it. When I reached the girl, I saw her face, round and pretty with nice even features, her eyes a blue glass, dazed and staring. I got behind her, locked an arm around her neck and started for shore with her. Her body relaxed at once and she let me take over, resting her head back in the water. I glanced again at her eyes. They were on the edge of going into shock.

The Rhine, at that point, not far below the swift and dangerous *gebirgsstrecke* or mountain stretch, still had a swift, powerful current. We were a couple of hundred yards downriver from where I'd left the car when I finally pulled the girl ashore. Her dress, a pink cotton print, was pressed tightly against her wet skin, revealing a thoroughly lovely full figure and large breasts with a certain self-sufficient majesty to them. A long but rounded torso had just enough waistline to be curvaceous and enough abdomen to be sensuous. Her face, very German, was classic in its broad cheekbones, fair complexion and small, upturned nose. The blue eyes were still in another world, though I thought I saw signs of them coming about. I could hear the whine of sirens and the sounds of voices as people flocked down to the riverbank. The girl's full breasts rose and fell in delicious rhythm as she breathed deep, air-gulping draughts. Small boats were putting out from shore to seek survivors. It would be a fruitless search, I was convinced. It had been one helluva explosion. I could still see that cabin being launched into the air like something from Cape Kennedy.

The girl stirred and I reached out to pull her up to a sitting position, the wet dress clinging to her, outlining every curve of her young body. The glassy-eyed look had vanished and had been replaced by a moment of remembrance, a sudden return of horror flooding back into her consciousness. I saw the fear and panic leap into her eyes and I reached out for her. She tumbled into my arms, wet softness, shuddering sobs wracking her body.

"Nein, Fräulein," I murmured. *"Kein mehr, Schreien sie nicht. Alles ist über."*

I let her cling to me until her shaking sobs subsided and she drew back, her blue eyes searching my face.

"You saved my life. Thank you," she said.

"You probably would have made it to shore," I told her. I meant it. She might have.

"You were aboard the ship?" she half-questioned.

"No, sweetie," I answered. "I was driving alongside you when the explosion occurred. In fact, I was on my way to Koblenz to board her to meet a friend. I dived in, found you and got you to shore."

She looked around, and the fright was still very much in her eyes as she glanced out at the river, then peered up the sloping shoreline of the riverbank. She shivered in the wet cotton as a wind blew and the dress, pressed against her, outlined the small buttons of her nipples. She turned to catch my eyes on them and I saw her own blue pupils flicker ever so slightly.

"My name is Helga," she said. "Helga Ruten."

"And I'm Nick Carter," I said.

"You are not German?" she asked in surprise. "You speak a magnificent German."

"American," I said. "Did you have anyone else aboard with you, Helga?"

"No, I was alone," she said. "It was a pleasant afternoon and I'd just decided to go for the sail."

Her eyes were studying me now, flicking across my chest and shoulders. There was over six feet of me for her to examine and it took her a few moments. Now it was my turn to see approval in her eyes. She kept her eyes averted from the scene of death and destruction in mid-river and made a remarkable recovery. Her eyes were clear, bright, her voice even and controlled. She was shivering, but from the cold, wet clothes.

"You say you have a car here?" she asked and I nodded, gesturing back up the bank.

"I have an uncle who has a home nearby," she said. "In fact, I was just admiring it when . . . when it happened. I know where the key is kept. We could go there and dry out."

"Fine with me," I said, helping her to her feet. She swayed, came against me and her breasts were soft and exciting against my skin, even through the wet cotton dress. This was a helluva lot of girl, I decided. I was never more right. I went back to the car with her, threw my things in the back seat and took a final look at the rescuers now crowding the river. Most of what they had to do would come under the name of classifying and recovering. It had been a thoroughly nasty piece of business, and I thought about Ted Dennison. Maybe he had survived, but it was unlikely. I rather thought Helga was just about the only survivor or damn near it. I'd check the police and the hospitals when I got to a phone and get in touch with Hawk later. Poor Ted, to live a lifetime with death and danger and then get it because the boiler of an excursion boat blows up.

Helga was shaking from the wet and the cold now. She pointed to the top of an old *schloss* rising majestically out of the mountains not far ahead.

"Turn off here at the first exit and take the small road at the end of it . . . *Zauber Gässchen,*" she said.

"Enchanted Lane," I repeated. "Nice name."

"It is a private road," she went on. "It leads to the door of my uncle's castle. The castle grounds run right to the river. Uncle has a landing there but he only uses the place on weekends really. He's not one of these broken-down nobility who have to turn their places into sight-seeing stops or museums. He's an industrialist."

I found the little road marked Enchanted Lane, followed it up through thickly wooded terrain. As the road wound its way steeply, I caught glimpses of huge, open expanses of green lawn enclosed by heavy woods. Helga was shivering almost continuously now, and as we moved upwards I felt the change in the air, felt my own skin growing cold and rough. I was glad when I found myself staring at the drawbridge of the huge moated castle, grim and forbidding as it was. Helga told me I could drive across the drawbridge and I did so, halting before the huge wooden door. She hopped out and hunted around some of the big blocks of stone at the corner of the high wall surrounding the castle. She came up with a set of large, heavy, iron keys, inserted one into the lock and the huge door swung slowly open just as I was getting out to help her.

Hopping back into the car, she said, "Drive right into the court and let's get out of these wet things."

"Right," I answered, tooling the little Opel into the huge, empty stone courtyard where once rows of knights and their squires lined up.

"Does your uncle happen to have a telephone?" I asked Helga.

"Oh, yes," she said, running both hands through her shock of very blond hair, tossing her head to shake the wetness out. "There are phones all over the place."

"Good," I said. "I told you I was boarding the excursion boat to meet an old business acquaintance. I want to find out what happened to him."

There was an eerie quiet to the huge castle as I stood in my shorts in the courtyard, looking up at the turreted walls, the ancient stone battlements.

"No servants?" I asked Helga.

"Uncle has them come only on the weekends when he's here," she said. "There's a gardener somewhere about and a wine cellar man, but that's all.

Come, I'll show you to a room where you can dry out."

She led me past the huge main hall where I glimpsed two long oak tables and medieval banners hanging from the ceiling, stone walls and a huge fireplace. The room she led me into was a tremendous place in itself with a king-size canopied bed, rich draperies and tapestries and high-backed, sturdy chairs of wood with thick brocade pillows. A tall credenza stood at one end and from it, Helga tossed me a towel.

"It's a kind of guest room," she said, gesturing to the walls. "I've stayed in it myself. I'll be down the corridor, changing. See you in five minutes."

I watched her go, wet dress still pressed tightly against a round, slightly plump rear. Helga, I'd decided, was a big girl on a big frame, but she carried it all off exceedingly well. I dried myself thoroughly, put back on everything but my jacket and stretched out on the huge bed. I had just about concluded that I was living in the wrong century when Helga reappeared in tight tan jeans and a deep-brown blouse tucked up and tied in front to give her a bare midriff. I was astounded at her appearance. I've known babes who would've been in bed with the shakes for a week after having gone through what she had just lived through. Helga, blond hair combed out in thick yellow cascades, blue eyes sparkling, bore no trace of the ordeal.

"I forgot, you wanted to use the phone," she said,

smiling warmly. "It's under the bed. I'll be downstairs in the main hall. Come down when you're finished." I watched her walk out, the jeans tight around her buttocks, forming a kind of girdle of their own, her walk a slow, gliding movement. I quickly decided that this century was good enough for me and reached under the bed for the phone.

II

It was grim and it was painfully slow, but I stuck with it. I checked out every hospital and aid station in the area. I was damn near at the end of the list when I got the message I didn't want to hear. Ted Dennison's body had been recovered and identified. There were only four survivors besides Helga, it seemed, two men, a woman and a child. Grimly, I put in an overseas call, collect, for Hawk and managed to get through unusually quickly. After I told him of the tragic accident, there was a long pause and then his voice, flat and icy, tossed one out at me.

"It was no accident," he said. That was all. He just threw it out and let it lie there, knowing I'd pick up the chill meaning.

"You sure of that?" I asked, a little gruffly.

"If you mean proof, you know better," Hawk answered. "If you mean am I convinced, I'm damn well certain of it."

As he spoke, something kept popping up in my mind. I kept seeing the boat opposite me and hearing the explosions. There had definitely been two of them, in instant succession, but two nonetheless. The smaller one first, immediately followed by the huge roar as the boilers went up. Two explosions. I heard them again in my mind, this time with a new meaning.

"They killed all those people just to get at Ted," I said, a little awed by the monstrousness of the thought.

"To keep him from talking to you," Hawk said. "Besides, what's a few hundred innocent lives to some people? Hell, Nick, don't tell me you're shocked at that anymore, after all these years in the business."

The Chief was right, of course. I shouldn't have been shocked. I'd seen it before, the callous disregard for life, the slaughter of the innocent, the end justifying the means. Long ago I'd come to learn that those who believed themselves touched by destiny always seemed to adopt a terrible indifference to the importance of human life. No, I wasn't really shocked in the true sense of the word. Appalled was probably a better term, appalled and angered. And there was one other inescapable conclusion.

"Whatever Ted found out," I said to Hawk, "was important. They're taking no chances, it seems."

"Which means it's important to us, too," Hawk said. "I'm going to meet you in West Berlin tomorrow, at our place. You know the present set-up there. I'll catch a plane tonight and be there in the morning. I'll fill you in on what little we know at that time."

I put down the phone and felt a hard knot of anger growing in my stomach. Strangely enough, though I felt very bad about Ted Dennison, it was the others that really got to me. Ted was a professional, like myself. We lived with death. We laughed, loved, ate and slept with death. We were fair game. If they wanted to get to Ted they should have found a way to reach just him. But they had taken the easy way, the callous way. And in doing so, they had involved me, Nick Carter, the human being as well as agent N3. Whoever they were, they'd be sorry. I could promise them that.

I got up from the wide bed, opened the heavy door and stepped outside into the gloomy, dank, stone corridor. Suddenly I knew I wasn't alone. I felt eyes boring into my back. I whirled but I could only see dim shadows. Still, I sensed the presence of another person. Then I saw the man, at the far end of the corridor, tall, well built, sandy colored hair. He had small blue eyes and a thin slit of a mouth. He didn't look like a gardener, nor did he look like any little old winekeeper I'd ever seen. He watched me for a moment, then slipped away through one of the numerous archways that led from the corridor. I turned and walked to the main hall where Helga sat with her legs irreverently propped up on one of the long oak tables.

"I just saw someone," I said. "Back there in the corridor."

"Oh, you saw Kurt." She smiled. "The watchman. I'd forgotten about him. Nowadays you need someone always on the premises as a guard."

She stood up and came over to me, taking both my hands in hers. I knew she saw my eyes dwell on those absolutely magnificent full breasts straining the thin fabric of the tucked-up blouse. I told her about finding out that my friend had been killed in the explosion and she was appropriately sympathetic. When I told her about having to be in West Berlin in the morning, Helga broke out in a warm, dazzling smile.

"That's wonderful," she exclaimed, pressing my hands tightly. "I live in West Berlin. We can spend the night here at the castle and drive in in the morning. It'll be night soon and why drive after dark? Besides, I'd love to cook a meal for you here. Please, you must let me."

"I don't want to be a bother," I said, a little weakly, I'm afraid. The idea of spending the night with this very open, outgoing girl had more than a little appeal. I didn't plan on anything but pleasant company, but I'd also learned that one never knows when opportunity will knock. And if Helga knocked, it would be a sin not to answer.

"You wouldn't be a bother," she was saying, bringing my attention back from those jutting contours. "You saved my life, remember? You deserve a lot more than just a dinner. But let's start with that first."

Helga, I was rapidly finding out, was one of those girls who said things which could be interpreted in six different ways and then instantly proceeded onto something else, leaving you with no further clues to help you interpret correctly.

"Come," she said, taking my hand. "Sit in the kitchen with me while I start dinner. We can talk there."

The kitchen turned out to be a vast but obviously well-functioning establishment with great copper and stainless steel kettles hanging from the ceiling on long hooks. A rack of pots and pans crisscrossed the kettles and one entire wall held stacks of dishes, roasting pans and cutlery. Uncle, I decided, threw some sizable bashes over the weekends. A huge, old-fashioned stone oven lined one wall, and a freezer provided a jarring note of modernity. Helga extracted a side of beef from it, took a huge knife and deftly sliced away. In no time at all she had various pots and pans simmering and brewing and the big oven ablaze. While working, as I sat in a wide-backed comfortable chair, she told me she was a secretary in West Berlin, that she was originally from Hanover and that she liked the good life.

When she reached a certain point in the proceedings, she steered me to a small bar off the main hall and suggested I fix drinks. Then, with drinks in hand, she gave me a tour of the castle. Walking with her arm in mine, her thigh rubbing warmly against mine at every other step, she was a most provocative guide. The castle, I noted, had a number of small rooms on the second and third floors of the main section or keep, as they call it. Various medieval hardware adorned the walls, and the staircases were the ancient, stone, unbannistered, spiraling steps. I glimpsed a large room on the second floor which had been modernized with rows of bookshelves and a desk. She referred to it as her uncle's study. Helga kept up a perfectly pleasant line of chatter and small talk and I found myself wondering if she did it to prevent me from noting that she kept away from the entire left half of the second story where I saw three rooms tightly closed. If that had been her intent, it didn't work. The three rooms were almost conspicuous because of their grim, closed contrast to the rest of the place. Downstairs, I mentioned wanting to see the wine cellar and I thought I noticed her hesitate for just a moment. It was fleeting and I wasn't sure, but I wondered about it.

"Of course, the wine cellar," she smiled, leading me down a narrow flight of stone steps. Great round casks stood in silent rows, each one with its own little wooden spigot and each one sporting a tag on which the date and classification of the wine had been marked. It was a big wine cellar with rows on rows of the huge casks. As we went back upstairs, something bothered me but I had no idea what it was. My mind had always worked in that strange way, sending out little signals of its own that only clarified themselves later on. But they acted as a series of mental reference points that usually came in more than handy at the right time. This was a perfect example. It had been a completely normal-appearing wine cellar, and yet I was bothered by something. I put it aside, knowing there was no use thinking about it at the moment. Back in the kitchen, I watched Helga finish preparing dinner.

"You know, Nick, you're the first American I've ever really known," she said. "I've seen a number of American tourists, of course, but they don't count. And none of them looked like you. You're an exceptionally handsome man."

I had to smile. False modesty was never for me. Helga stretched.

"Do you find me attractive?" she asked openly. In court that would have been called leading the witness. I watched her breasts stand out as she flexed her arms behind her head.

"Attractive isn't the word, honey," I told her. She smiled and took down a stack of plates.

"Dinner's almost ready," she said. "Make us another drink while I set the table and change."

After the second round of drinks, we dined at one end of the long table, by candlelight, with a fire in the big fireplace. Helga had changed into a black velvet dress with buttons that buttoned at the end of a series of loops running down the front to her waist. The loops were wide and beneath each of them was Helga and nothing else. The dress, V-necked, struggled hard to keep Helga's breasts inside. Happily, it was not an altogether successful struggle. She had produced two bottles of superb local wine, not from the castle vineyards, she said, explaining that her uncle bottled very little, but sold mostly "from the wood" to other bottlers. Dinner was excellent and after the food, drinks and wine, a cozy rapport had built up between Helga and myself. She downed a good brandy, an armagnac, as we sat on a curved sofa before the fireplace. The night had turned cool and the huge castle was dank and damp, so the fire made a welcome oasis of warmth.

"Is it true," Helga asked, "that they are still very puritan in America in regard to sex?"

"Puritan?" I questioned. "How do you mean that?"

She toyed with her brandy snifter, peering up at me over the edge of it. "I heard that American girls still feel they must make excuses for wanting to go to bed with a man," she said idly. "They still feel they must say they're in love, or they had too much to drink, or they were feeling sorry for him or some such nonsense. And American men still expect them to make such excuses or they think the girl is a tramp."

I had to smile. There was a lot of truth in what she was saying.

"Would you feel a girl was a tramp if she didn't cloak her feelings in such ridiculous pretexts?" Helga went on.

"No," I answered. "But then I'm not really the average American male."

"No, of course not," she murmured, her eyes wandering across my face. "I think you're not average anywhere. There is something about you I have never met in any other man. It is as though you can be terribly sweet and terribly cruel."

"You speak about the pretexts and excuses of American girls, Helga. I take it you're saying the average German girl doesn't need excuses."

"Not so much anymore," Helga said, turning fully toward me, her breasts soft white mounds pushing over the top of the black velvet. "We have finished with excuses here. We face the truth of our human needs and desires for what they are. Maybe it is a result of all the wars and the suffering, but today we do not fool ourselves anymore. We recognize power as power, greed as greed, weakness as weakness, strength as strength, sex as sex. Here a girl does not expect a man to say I love you when he means I want you. And a man does not expect a girl to hide her own desires behind silly pretenses."

"Very enlightened and commendable," I said. Helga's eyes had turned a smoky, cloudy blue and they kept flicking from my face, down across my body and then back again. Her lips, slightly parted, were wet as she drew her tongue slowly back and forth across them. Her obvious desire was an electric current setting my own body aflame. I reached out and put one hand behind her neck, squeezing firmly, moving her toward me slowly.

"And when you have desires, Helga," I said quietly, very quietly. "What do you say?" Her lips parted further and she came toward me. I felt her arms slide around my neck.

"I say I want you," she murmured huskily, just barely audibly. "I say I want you."

Her lips were against mine, soft and yielding, wet and smooth. I felt her mouth open and her tongue shot out, flicking back and forth. I moved my hand down and the loops of the dress parted instantly and Helga's breast was soft against my palm.

She put her head back for an instant, tearing her lips from mine, and her body straightened out with a sudden quiver, her legs pushing forward. Her breasts were deep and full, I saw, soft white with small pink tips that rose at once to the touch. All the loops of the dress had come open and Helga had slipped out of it entirely. She wore only black bikini panties and as I pressed my lips down on her softly yielding breasts, she drew her legs up in an involuntary reaction. She thrust upwards, pushing her breasts toward my mouth, and her hands were quivering and clutching at me. She was panting and making small, unintelligible sounds of pleasure, her arms convulsively tightening and releasing.

I stood up and undressed, starting with my shirt. It was both slow and pleasurable, for Helga clung to me as I undressed, running her hands up and down my torso, pressing her face against my stomach, clutching my body to her. I took both full breasts in my hands and moved them in a slow, circular motion. Helga put her blond head back and moaned softly. I traced a slow, lambent line of pleasure down her torso with my tongue until her moans turned to cries of ecstasy. Helga became a quivering, pulsating wire, arching her back, thrusting herself upwards, begging with her hips for the moment she hungered for with such absolute abandon. And it was indeed abandon, but of a strange sort. There was none of the utter freedom and ecstatic delight, the pure pleasure of letting oneself completely succumb to the senses. It was an abandon that seemed to explode from some inner drive, from some tremendous need.

Helga's hips were wide and heavy boned. Fitting against them was both comfortable and somehow very proper. There was something of the earth goddess about her figure and her all-consuming manner. As I answered her moans and cries of desire with my body, she stiffened for an instant and then began to thrust herself up and down, her legs locked around my back. I felt carried away on some Valkyrian ride into the skies. Helga moaned and sobbed and cried and sighed, her breasts under my hands tossing and turning, her lips not kissing but sucking against my shoulder, moving down to my chest. Her tremendous drive was all embracing as well as all consuming, and I felt myself carried along with it, matching her every thrust with my own body until the wide, heavy sofa shook. Then, with a suddenness that surprised me, she pressed herself against me, hands digging into my back as a long, shuddering sob wracked her body. "Oh, God Almighty," she said, tearing the words out of her inner depths and then falling backwards to lie there, legs still locked around me, her large breasts heaving. She took my hand and placed it on one breast while her stomach, soft and round, slowly began to cease its contractions.

Finally I lay beside her and realized I was having a very odd reaction to what had happened. It had been exciting, unquestionably. And very pleasurable, too. I'd enjoyed every moment of it and yet I felt strangely unsatisfied. Somehow, I didn't feel that I had made love to Helga, that it was I who had brought her to new heights of sensual pleasure. Instead, I had the distinct feeling that I had been an object, something she had used to gratify herself. As I lay there, taking in the full contours of her body, I knew I wanted to make love to her again some other time, to see if the same, strange reaction came across. It would be worth it for itself, but this added to my desire. Of course, I knew that the first time, despite the qualities it always brought along, was never the most satisfactory with any woman. To bring the most out of a woman one has to learn how her sensory and psychic centers react and this takes time. Helga stirred and sat up, stretching, her arms upraised, lifting her gorgeous, full breasts in supplication.

"I'm going up to my room to go to bed," she announced, getting to her feet.

"Alone?" I asked.

"Alone," she said to my surprise, flatly and matter-of-factly. "I can't stand to sleep with anyone. Good night, Nick."

She got up, came before me, pressed one breast into my face for an instant and then was gone, hurrying across the room, a ghost-like white form in the deep shadows. I stayed and watched the fire for a while and then went up to the room where I'd dried off. I went to sleep in the huge bed thinking that Helga was a most unusual girl. I had the thought that she was far from representative of the average *fräulein*.

In the morning I woke early. The great *schloss* was silent as a tomb. During the night I'd woken with a start at what I thought was a scream of pain. I'd sat up, listening in the dark, and there had been only silence. It could well have been a dream, I knew, and I went back to sleep. Nothing further happened to wake me and I slept the rest of the night soundly. I half-dressed and started down to get my shaving kit from the car. The door to Helga's room was ajar and I peered in. She was still asleep, the covers at her waist, her breasts two snowy peaks, her blond hair a golden circle on the pillow. She was a very striking dish, I realized once again. Striking and unusual, a fascinating combination for any man. But when I'd finished shaving, I knew that the day would be far too crowded to think much about Helga. I was on my way back to Helga's room to wake her when I found the feather in the corridor, long, brown with black spots. I'd seen feathers like this one before and I was trying to remember where and when. I was studying it when Helga appeared, dressed in the cotton print again, which, dried out, had a full, saucy line to it. I held the feather out to her.

"All kinds of birds fly in here," she said, coming up to press herself against me, her lips smooth and warm on mine. Her hands were moving down my waist. "I wish we could stay," she murmured. I dropped the feather and held her close.

"Me, too," I said. "And cut it out. You're only making it worse." Helga smiled and stepped back. Her hand found mine and we went down to the courtyard and the little Opel. As we drove down the winding lane, back onto the main road, I saw she was wearing a smile that went beyond contentment, a smile that was of satisfaction. A most unusual girl, this Helga Ruten, I decided once again and as I drove toward West Berlin my thoughts kept returning to the night before. It had been the first night I'd ever slept as a guest in a castle and, as I thought about it, I realized that for all the times Helga had mentioned her uncle, I knew nothing at all about the man. I thought of asking his name, but I decided against it. It had been a lovely interlude. Why probe further? Hawk would be meeting me in a few hours with God knows what assignment. Helga would be a lovely memory. And if I did see her again, there'd be plenty of time to bring it up then.

We reached Helmstedt, the checkpoint for all traffic from West Germany on the *Autobahn,* in good time. My papers were checked and passed. Helga had her residence identification from West Berlin. From Helmstedt to West Berlin on the *Autobahn* came out to exactly 104 miles of fairly bumpy road. I decided the *Autobahn* could stand some repairs. The only good thing was the unlimited speed possibilities. The little car went as fast as it could and was a hot, grinding thing when we reached West Berlin where, after a final check by the *Vopos,* the East German *Volkspolizei* or People's Police, we were passed on through. Once inside West Berlin, an oasis of freedom surrounded by the Communist sea of East Germany, Helga directed me to her place not far from Tempelhof Airport. She swung her young sturdy legs out of the car and came around to the driver's side. She took out a key ring, snapped a key from it and handed it to me.

"If you're staying on in West Berlin," she said, her blue eyes impassive. "It'll be cheaper than a hotel."

"If I stay, you can count on it," I said, dropping the key into my pocket. She turned and walked away, her hips swinging. I watched her walk into 27 Ulme Strasse, put the little Opel into gear and took off before I decided to follow her. The key in my pocket burned with a delightful anticipation that I was confident my meeting with Hawk would extinguish. I headed for Kurfürstendamm Strasse and AXE headquarters in West Berlin.

III

My rented car had been pushed beyond its endurance, and it was sounding more and more like a coffee grinder as I headed for West Berlin's Fifth Avenue, Kurfürstendamm Strasse. I'd switched off Helga and it was a different me now. Strictly business, every sense turned on to full. It was always like that with me. There came a moment, a time, an instant when agent N3 took over completely. It was partly training and partly some inner mechanism which seemed to switch on by itself. Maybe it was triggered by the scent of danger or the anticipation of combat or the excitement of the chase. I don't really know, except that it always happened and I could feel the difference come over me. Whether it was this heightened alertness or just a matter of habit, but as I checked my rear-view mirror I suddenly realized something. I had picked up a tail. Traffic was heavy and I'd cut through a number of side streets to try and make time and whenever I glanced through my mirror I saw the Lancia two or three cars back. It was a steel-gray, powerful job, about a 1950 vintage, I guessed, that could hit a hundred with ease. It was a car whose performance fifteen years ago was not really outdone by today's models. I turned a few more corners. My suspicions were right. The Lancia was still there, a good tail, staying a few cars back so as not to arouse suspicion. They didn't know it, but I was easily aroused and naturally suspicious.

At first I wondered how in hell they had gotten onto me so quickly. Then, as I thought back, I realized that they could have picked me up at a number of spots, entering East Germany, at the West Berlin checkpoint, or even when I rented the Opel back in Frankfurt. That wouldn't surprise me now. I was getting grimly respectful of this bunch, whoever they were. They had a helluva network and they had shown themselves to be ruthless and efficient. And now they were sticking with me, waiting for me to lead them to AXE headquarters here in West Berlin. Like hell, friends, I angrily answered them. That was one thing I wouldn't do, even if it meant my not showing up.

I pushed the little Opel into a traffic circle, went around it twice and then cut off down a narrow street. The Lancia had to cut sharply and almost didn't make the corner, I noted with satisfaction. I turned sharply at the next corner, and then left at the next. I could hear the Lancia's tires squeal on the sharp, narrow corners. If these narrow, twisting streets held out I could lose them. But they didn't hold out, I saw with an oath as I found myself on a broad street lined with warehouses and truck depots. Through the mirror I saw the Lancia open up. They knew now that I knew and they were no longer tailing me. They were after me, cutting around trucks and gaining fast. The Lancia's heavy chassis with big fenders and powerful bumpers could crush the little Opel like an eggshell. I knew the bit all too well. A collision, an accident and they took off to let the *polizei* wrestle with the remains.

The Opel was straining, making more noise and doing less and the damned depots lining the street seemed endless. There was no place to turn and the Lancia was coming up fast. Suddenly I saw it, a narrow cut between two of the depots. I swerved, hearing the tires howl in protest as the car leaned over. One fender hit a corner of a loading platform on one of the depots, putting a deep gash in it, but I had made the passageway, tissue-paper to spare on each side. I hadn't heard the Lancia brake to a screeching halt, which bothered me. I found out why when I came out at the end of the passageway to see the steel-gray car hurtle around a corner two blocks below. I saw they had another advantage. They knew West Berlin far better than I did.

I was on another wide street and saw the Lancia barreling up to me again. I started to cut across to a group of side streets, but suddenly realized I was out of time. The Lancia would go into me broadside at full speed. I wrenched the wheel the other way just as the heavier car hurtled up, catching my rear fender and sending the little Opel spinning like a top. The Lancia had overshot and had to brake and back up. I came out of the spin gunning the Opel forward across the wide street and into one of the narrower side streets. I heard the Lancia's engines roar as they took after me again. I hadn't been able to get a look at the occupants of the Lancia, but I saw there were at least three, perhaps four, men.

I swung out of the side street into an area of warehouses and open-air grocery markets. People and cars were lined up outside the grocery markets and I snaked my way through them, catching a glimpse of the Lancia emerging from the side street. Once again, the tight areas gave my little car a temporary advantage that I knew would evaporate as soon as the Lancia threaded its way through the crowds. I pointed the Opel toward a big, square, drab building with boarded-up windows and skidded to a halt alongside two wide, overhead delivery doors that were shut. I glanced back to see the Lancia, headed straight for me, gathering speed. I dived out the door opposite the driver's seat, hitting the ground and rolling over just as the crash resounded. I looked up to see the Opel flattened against the heavy steel warehouse doors. I saw the Lancia, as it backed off, was not only heavier, but carried a reinforced front end that was without damage except for some crumpled metal.

I had seen the smaller entrance alongside the heavy overhead steel doors and my shoulder hit it just as they pegged the first shot at me. It flew open and I paused to glance back. I'd been right, there were four of them tumbling out of the Lancia. I decided to let Wilhelmina slow them down a little. One shot did it, scattering them like leaves in a sudden gust of wind as I ran into the building. It was more of a cold storage depot than an active warehouse, a dim, cavernous building with rows upon rows of crates, bales and boxes piled atop each other. A network of steel ladders and catwalks led to open sided floors of steel where more boxes and crates were stacked. My thought had been to simply race through the building and out the rear. It had been a good enough idea except that there was no rear exit. Everything was barred and boarded up tight. I heard the sounds of voices and footsteps and I flattened myself against one of the rows of crates. They were separating, fanning out to find me. Textbook strategy, but unimaginative and it could backfire. I heard one of them moving down the corridor toward me, hurrying, being incautious. I would have taken him quickly, quietly and easily with one blow from Wilhelmina when a floorboard creaked beneath my foot just as he came opposite me. He whirled and I was surprised. I'd expected a big German or perhaps a burly Russian. This one was short, black haired and dark complexioned with a prominent, beaked nose. I saw him start to bring up his right hand, saw the gun in it and I swung, connecting solidly right on the point of the jaw. He went down in a heap, but not before the gun went off, the shot echoing off the walls of the warehouse.

Other footsteps were running toward me at once and I ducked down one of the passageways between the crates, cut through another one and dived behind a third stack. I heard them get the one to his feet and then they spread out along one of the corridors so they could work their way back together. I looked behind and saw that I could move back, but it would only be a delaying action. In minutes I'd be up against the barred and boarded rear wall and out of hiding and running space. The crates in front of me were stacked up in step-like fashion. Reaching up, I pulled myself up onto the nearest ones and then I climbed onto the top row. Lying flat, I edged myself across the tops of the crates until I reached the forward edge and looked down onto the corridors below. They were advancing slowly, carefully peering around the corners of each cross passageway. Two of them were blond and big as I'd expected. The other two were smaller, black haired and swarthy.

If I were going to get out of this it wouldn't be by an exchange of gunfire. I'd only end up trapping myself into a gun battle in which the odds were four to one and my position would be pinned down. The warehouse had turned out to be something of a cul-de-sac and I had to get out as quickly as possible. As I pulled myself over it, one of the crates teetered. I drew back and looked down at the searchers. One of the blond ones was just underneath. I rapidly calculated the distance between the rows of crates as about four feet. It was worth a try and it would take them by surprise. That element was the thing I needed to give me even a few sceonds jump on them.

I pushed hard on the top crate. It toppled over, perfectly on target. But the sound of its scraping over the edge of the crate beneath it gave the man a chance to look up and duck away. Nevertheless, it caught him a glancing blow that sent him sprawling in pain, clutching his shoulder as he hit the floor. I leaped across the chasm separating the rows of crates, landing on my feet atop the opposite row. I made no effort to be silent now, as I raced across the tops of the boxes and bales. Speed was the essential thing. I judged the next leap without stopping and took it on the run, this time landing on my hands and knees. I scrambled down the sides of the crates to the floor and raced for the entrance. I could hear them racing after me, but the few seconds of surprise had given me the jump on them I needed. I was outside and racing across the cobblestones before they reached the door. A group of curious people were gathered around the flattened wreck of the Opel, no doubt waiting for the cops to arrive on the scene, The Lancia, a grim, forbidding symbol, stood waiting.

Glancing back, I saw three of them now coming after me. I was heading for the open-air grocery market stalls, hoping I'd lose myself in the crowd, when I saw the girl just getting into the Mercedes 250SL coupe with an armload of groceries. It was just what I needed. The car, not the girl. The Mercedes, I knew, could outrun the Lancia. The girl, I saw in one fast, sweeping glance, was pretty, lithe and tall, wearing a light gray sweater and pearl-gray slacks. I reached the car just as she opened the door at the driver's side and started to get in. She turned, alarm in her hazel eyes as I shoved in beside her pushing her from behind the wheel.

"Be quiet," I growled at her. "I won't hurt you." Not on purpose, I added to myself. I realized I'd spoken in English and started to translate into German when she interrupted.

"I understand English," she snapped. "What is this?"

I switched the engine on, hearing the sweet, full roar of the Mercedes power plant.

"Nothing," I said, sending the Mercedes coupe roaring directly at the three men. They scattered, diving for the protection of the Lancia as I took off past them. The girl glanced back, seeing the Lancia immediately come to life and start after us.

"Stop this at once," she commanded crisply.

"Sorry," I said, sending the Mercedes around a corner on two wheels.

"You're not German," she said. "You're American. What are you running from? What are you, an Army deserter?"

"No," I said, taking another corner on the side of the tires. "But this isn't quiz time, honey. Save it."

I saw her glance back at the pursuing Lancia. I'd come upon an open stretch and pressed the accelerator, feeling the Mercedes leap forward. I smiled.

"I'm glad you're happy," the girl said with asperity. "Where are you going? What are you going to do with me?"

"Nothing," I said. "Relax."

"And leave the driving to you," she added. I shot her a quick glance. She was very pretty, I saw, with a pert, saucy face that was extremely cool and self-contained. Her breasts were filling the sweater without effort. I was going to ask her where she'd learned that kind of American jargon when the shot pinged across the roof of the car.

"Get down!" I yelled at her and she promptly slid to the floor, looking up at me.

"I'm not relaxed," she said.

"Neither am I," I answered, careening around another corner. She was a very cool customer, I saw. She was studying me from her spot on the floor with the calmness she might have used in a living room. Another shot grazed the roof of the Mercedes. They realized that there was little chance of their overtaking me. Their only resort now was to stop me. The avenue had swung around so that we were paralleling a half-dozen sets of railroad tracks on what was apparently a service road. A fast passenger train powered by a diesel engine hurtled past in the opposite direction. So did an idea. I was beginning to conclude that I couldn't really shake my pursuers, even with the Mercedes, here in the city. There were just too many turns and twists and traffic obstacles. I needed a highway to outrun them and there wasn't one around. But there was something I could do and the first step was to put some more space between the Lancia and myself. I gunned the Mercedes and saw the girl, still crouched on the floor, stiffen as we sped along the avenue, swerving and slipping past other cars by inches, avoiding collisions by split seconds.

"Why don't you give yourself up?" she asked. "It's better than being dead. You'll kill us both."

"You do just as I say and you'll be all right," I answered her. I was overtaking a speeding express train and I could read the sign on the side of the cars: BERLIN-HAMBURG-SCHNELIZUG. It was a fast train, all right. I had to hit over a hundred to pass it. The Lancia had dropped back out of sight temporarily, but I knew they were still there. I saw the girl's saucy face watching me with eyes narrowed. It was going to be a close one, I knew. As the railroad crossing came into view, not more than a mile ahead, I kicked the Mercedes up still further, watching the speedometer needle climb to 115. We were almost at the crossing. I shot a glance back at the express.

"Get on the seat," I yelled at the girl, saw her pull herself up. "When I say so, you dive out of this car and run forward across the tracks, understand? And, baby, you better move or you won't be around to ask any more questions."

She didn't answer. She didn't need to. She had taken in the hurtling diesel just back of us and the upcoming crossing. My hands were wet on the wheel, my fingers cramped. I flexed my right hand, then my left, took another grip on the wheel. We were at the crossing point. I swung the Mercedes, braking only enough to avoid turning over and skidded to a halt dead on the tracks. The diesel was not more than a hundred feet away, a huge behemoth with not the ghost of a chance of stopping.

"Out!" I yelled at the girl and I saw she was already opening the door. I watched her rear end disappear out the door as I followed after her. I did a rolling somersault and was back on my feet before she was. I grabbed her hand, yanked her to her feet and started to run with her. We had just cleared the tracks when the locomotive plowed into the Mercedes. The day lit up with a ball of flame that scorched my back and knocked me forward. The sound of tearing, rending metal screeched through the explosion. The girl yanked her hand free and

stopped to look back at the twisted, burning mass still being pushed by the diesel.

"My car!" she cried out in dismay.

"I'll get you a new one," I said, grabbing her hand and yanking her along. By now the Lancia had reached the scene, I knew, and was halted on the other side of the tracks, its occupants convinced I had misjudged and was inside the wreckage, rapidly on my way to becoming a cinder. I smiled in satisfaction and finally paused as we reached an intersection a few blocks away. It would take them hours to clear the tracks.

I looked at the girl standing beside me, panting, trying to catch her breath, her face smudged and smeared from where she'd hit the roadbed by the tracks. I had the chance to really look at her now, and I found myself appreciating the nice, high line of her breasts, her long, lithe legs sheathed in the gray slacks. She maintained her cool, self-contained control and she was studying me with speculation dancing in her hazel eyes.

"You're no deserter," she said firmly. "I don't know what you are, but it's not that."

"Go to the head of the class," I said.

"Just what are you?" she asked. "Some kind of nut?"

"You speak a damned colloquial American for a German girl," I said with a frown.

"I go to a lot of American movies," she answered blandly.

"If you give me your name and address I'll see that you're reimbursed for your car," I told her. She studied me as if she were eyeing some unbelievable object under a microscope. I wished I had the time to stay with her. She was not only extremely pretty, but there was a fascinating quality to her, an air of bemused assurance I'd never met before in a European girl.

"I don't believe all this," she said, her face creasing into a frown. "I know what just happened, because I was part of it, but I don't believe it. And now you're offering to pay for my car. Why don't you tell me who you are and what this is all about?"

"Because I don't have the time, for one thing, honey. You just give me your name and address and I'll see that you're reimbursed."

She shook her head again in disbelief. "I don't have the slightest idea why, but somehow I believe you," she said.

"I have an honest face," I grinned down at her.

"No, you have a fascinating face," she said. "But you could be anything from an avenging angel to a super jewel thief."

"You work on it, honey," I said. "Now, your name. I'm running very late."

"My name is Lisa," she said. "Lisa Huffmann. The car really belongs to my aunt. I'm here visiting her, but if you make the check out to me I'll endorse it over to her. That's Lisa Huffmann, three hundred Kaiserlautern Strasse."

"It's as good as done," I said, noting the fullness of her lower lip, the soft, appealing line of her mouth. She continued to keep her cool, contained posture.

"Five thousand five hundred and forty-six dollars," she announced calmly. "It was a brand-new car."

I grinned. I found myself deciding I wanted to see this cool, unperturbed little morsel again. Her parting shot nailed down my conclusion.

"And nine dollars and thirty cents worth of groceries," she added.

"Lisa, girl," I laughed, "I'm going to deliver this to you myself if I possibly can." I left her standing there on the corner, watching as I hailed a Volkswagen taxi. I waved to her out the window as the cab rolled away. She didn't wave back. She just stood there, arms folded across her high breasts, and watched me go off. I'd have been disappointed in her if she had waved.

IV

AXE headquarters in West Berlin was always a legitimate cover, functioning normally in every respect, its real purpose known to not more than two of those involved. In addition, as an extra precaution, the entire cover was shifted every nine months to a year. All top AXE agents were informed of the shifts as they occurred and of all necessary code and identity procedures. As I paid the cab, I looked up at the modest office building with its collection of name-plates and signs lining one wall. My eyes came to a halt at the bottom name—BERLIN BALLET SCHULE. In smaller letters underneath were the words: Direktor—Herr Doktor Prellhaus.

I smiled. That would be Howie Prailler, of course. Howie was in charge of establishing and maintaining all AXE covers in the European theater. He had a special line of contacts and a special kind of talent for it. We'd met a couple of times previously. I took the elevator up to a large, airy, bright studio where I found myself watching some fifteen young *fräuleins*, ranging in age from about twelve to twenty, exercising and bending, practicing ballet dips and whirls. I noted there were four young men also, and three teachers—two men and a woman. Everyone was clothed in leotards and tights and very intent on his work. I entered unnoticed, except for the smallish, brown-haired woman at a desk off to the side. She beckoned to me and I went over.

"I have an appointment with Herr Doktor," I said. "I'm here about the magazine story on the school."

I was careful to be very formal and proper. The Germans are sticky about titles. If it's Herr Doktor, you'd better damn well address him as Herr Doktor. It was part of a general European attitude toward imposing forms of address I always felt was a holdover from the days when titles meant something.

The woman picked up a phone, pressed a buzzer and spoke to someone. Then she smiled and looked up at me.

"Go right in," she said. "The other gentleman from the photographer's studio has already arrived. Down the hallway, the second door."

I followed her glance across the studio and saw a small corridor on the other side. Skirting swinging and kicking legs, I threaded my way through the embryonic ballerinas, found the second door down the corridor and entered a small office. An instant glance at the insulation of the door and ceiling told me it was soundproof. Hawk was sitting in a deep leather chair and Howie Prailler behind a small, plain desk. Hawk's instant, two-word question reflected both his years of experience and his concern.

"What happened?" he asked. I nodded to Howie who gave me a fast smile in return. His eyes, too, were deep with worry.

"I had company," I said to Hawk.

"So soon?" he asked, his gray eyes behind the rimless spectacle unblinking. Only his voice showed his surprise.

"Exactly what I said to myself," I agreed.

"You shook them before coming here, of course."

"No, they're waiting outside to meet you. I told them I'd bring you out."

Hawk ignored me. It was a technique of his, especially when he realized I had him one up.

"How did you shake them?" he asked blandly.

"They think I misjudged a race with the Berlin-Hamburg Express." He listened intently as I briefly recounted exactly what had happened.

"Close, N3," he commented when I'd finished.

"Too damned close," I agreed. "I wish I knew where they put a tail on me first."

"So would I," Hawk said. "I can see how they could have gotten onto Ted Dennison, but I can't fathom them tabbing you. Not yet, at least. This is very disturbing to me, N3."

"It didn't do much for my peace of mind either," I

commented. I saw Howie Prailler trying to suppress a grin. Hawk's steely gray eyes didn't flicker.

"Sit down, Nick," he said. "Let me tell you what we've got so far. Every time I look into this thing, I like it less. Does the name Heinrich Dreissig mean anything to you?"

I knew a little about the man, really not much more than anyone who reads the newspapers fairly regularly.

"He heads that new German political party," I answered. "I believe they call themselves the NSH."

"That's right, the *Neue Stadt Herrenvolk Party.* And you know what that translates into."

"Yes," I said. "The New State People's Party . . . roughly." It was a rough translation because there was no real one-word English equivalent for *herrenvolk.* The compound word, so loved by the Germans, took on a meaning of its own. Master people was not accurate. Neither was super people or elite. Perhaps upper people was closest and even that was inaccurate. But to the Germans, and anyone who knew German, it meant the superior people and smelled of the old Hitler Master Race routine without actually saying so; a neat piece of political footwork.

"Let me give you a little background," Hawk went on. "The NSH and Heinrich Dreissig have been around for a while as a kind of fringe group. About seven or eight months ago, they suddenly began to move out of the sidelines and into the main area. They stopped being a two-bit, fringe operation and mounted a very sizable campaign during the last election. So sizable, in fact, that they won 40 seats in the *Bundestag*. Now, that may not seem like much, but 40 seats out of 499 is damn near 10 per cent. From a group that had only held three seats it's a very dramatic jump. Now, from your knowledge of politics in our country, you know what that kind of thing takes."

I nodded. "It takes loot. Moolah. Dough. Money and a lot of it.

"Exactly," Hawk continued. "And since then they've tripled their party personnel, continued their propaganda step-up' and gained an estimated 500 per cent increase in party membership. Dreissig has been devoting more time to hard, political speeches and what we call fence-mending in the States. Frankly, we're afraid of Dreissig and his NSH for a number of reasons. We know they have some very neo-Nazi ideas. We know they are very nationalistic. We know they are clever enough to stay within bounds so they can't be slapped down . . . until they're ready for further moves. We also know that they could upset the very delicate balance of European relations between the Russians and ourselves, between East and West. It hangs on a very finely balanced scale now. The emergence of a strong neo-Nazi nationalistic party could cause undreamed of repercussions brought on by fright, suspicion or misjudgment. We can't have that. But we know the NSH and Dreissig are up to something. We have to know what it is. That's why it's vital we find out where they're getting all this new money. If we can find that out, it will tell us a lot about what they're planning."

"And that's what Ted had learned and was to pass on to me," I said, musing aloud.

"Correct, N3," Hawk answered. "And they made sure he wouldn't pass it on. But there's another man who I feel confident knows. In fact, I'd wager that he probably passed the information on to Ted. But he's an operative we have in East Germany . . . a sleeper. We can't risk moving him out. You'll have to go in and get to him."

"I understand the Russians are keeping a very tight check on all traffic to and from East Berlin," I said.

"They are. That's the problem we must first meet," Hawk said. "How to get you into East Berlin. All of this has hit so suddenly that we haven't quite figured that one out yet. I thought perhaps your fertile little mind might come up with an idea or two. Howie can get you almost any kind of false papers. That's not the problem. The sticky bit is to get you some reason for entry which won't subject you to careful scrutiny at the Brandenburg Gate or to observance after you get in. Howie will be working on it also. You two get together tomorrow morning. I've got to catch the six o'clock flight back tonight from Tempelhof."

Hawk stood up. "It's your kettle of fish to fry now,

N3," he said. "We must know where Dreissig is getting the money. Then we'll find out what his plans are."

"Before you go," I interjected, "give me a check for that girl's car."

"I'll send you one from the States," Hawk said gruffly. "I've got to make up vouchers and transfer the request for funds. Hell, I can't go around writing out five-thousand-dollar checks."

"You know damn well you can do just that," I said, smiling pleasantly. "And don't try to sell me a bill of goods. I know better."

I did know better. AXE has funds all over the world, enough for a variety of purposes and emergencies—hush money, bribe money, information money, unexpected-expenses funds and money for legitimate items such as Lisa Huffmann's car. The slush fund for the European area was drawn on a Swiss bank. That was why he couldn't get away with the poormouth routine with me, though he always gave it a try. Perhaps that was one of the underlying reasons why he and I had such a good working relationship. Both of us, each in our own way, always gave it the old college try. It was, and always had been, a subtle battle of wits and one-upmanship between two people who thoroughly respected each other. I knew Hawk always balked at shelling out AXE funds for what he liked to call the "careless and casual" attitude on the part of his crew. It wasn't anything personal, ever. He knew that his operatives were far from careless or casual. It was, I'd always suspected, the residue of a tight, New England upbringing.

"Why didn't you pick some girl with a Volkswagen?" he grumbled, taking out his checkbook. "You've got to do something about your expensive tastes, N3."

"I will, as soon as I stop living," I commented. When I reminded him to be sure and add the nine dollars and thirty cents for groceries, he looked up at me for a long minute, steel-gray eyes unblinking.

"We're lucky." I shrugged.

"How do you come to that?" he said slowly and evenly.

"She could have been shopping at *der Deutsche* equivalent of Tiffany's."

Hawk thrust the check at me with a grunt. "I suppose I should be happy you're alive," he said gruffly. "Try and be more careful next time, N3."

It was practically a maudlin statement for Hawk. I nodded. The old bear did have feelings. You just had to blast for them. I waved goodbye to Howie Prailler, made my way back past the stretching, kicking ballerinas and down to the street. When I'd put the check in my pocket, I had touched the key and thoughts of Helga leaped up at once. I'd been given an unexpected bonus, an extra night in West Berlin with Helga. Of course, I was expected to come up with a good way to get into East Berlin, but maybe Helga could be helpful there, too. She seemed to know her way around. But first, there was Lisa Huffmann. Lisa evoked a completely different set of thoughts. Even in the brief and hectic time I'd spent with her, she had exuded a rare sophistication which appealed to the intellect as well as the body. Helga, however, was pure body. There was that strange aspect I'd felt about our lovemaking that intrigued me, but that was still pure body.

I kept eyes sharply peeled as I walked a few blocks. Satisfied that I was not being tailed again, I hailed a cab and settled back in the seat. I watched the smart, glittering shops of Kurfürstendamm Strasse go by; they were the equal of any modern Western capital. It was indeed a fantastic accomplishment. At the end of World War II, 90 per cent of the buildings of the street were either demolished or severely damaged. Every street in the city was gutted. Not only had it all been rebuilt, but 200,000 new homes had been erected. Every scrap of rubble that was salvageable was used in the rebuilding. They city was indeed a phoenix that had risen out of its own fiery ashes. I couldn't help wonder about Heinrich Dreissig and his neo-Nazi party. It was unthinkable that today's Germans would permit that phoenix of hate to rise out of the past. Yet to many, the past had been unthinkable. But it had happened. We had reached 300 Kaiserlauten Strasse and I got out before a modest, middle-class apartment house. I examined the mailboxes in the foyer. A small card was scotch-taped onto one. "L. Huffmann & Detweiner," it read. I rang the bell and L. Huffmann came to the door in a soft, cream-white dress that clung deliciously to her, accentuating the long narrow line of her slender body. It did all right by her lovely breasts, too, revealing the graceful, upturned thrust of her bustline. I saw her eyes widen as they focused on me.

"Surprised?" I grinned.

"Yes . . . and no," she replied "I certainly didn't expect you back so soon."

"I haven't much time," I told her, handing her the check. "Thanks again for the use of the car."

Lisa Huffmann studied the check, a small frown furrowing her smooth, wide brow. It was a numbered check on a numbered account in the Swiss bank. You couldn't tell a thing from it.

"It's good," I said.

"Thank you," she answered, fastening me with a long, speculative look once again. "And you're still the man of mystery. I don't even know your name. Is that still *verboten?*"

I laughed. "I guess not," I said. "It's Nick . . . Nick Carter." I wanted to say more. I wanted to stay, but staying would only mean added distractions. Right now Helga was enough. Besides, I had a very ticklish job to do. But I did want to see this very appealing creature again. Her composed self-assurance was both challenging and refreshing.

"You'll note that the grocery money is included," I said calmly.

"I noted it," she answered.

"Look, I'd like the chance to explain to you when I can," I said. "How about tabling everything till then?"

"When will *then* be?"

"I can't answer that now, but I'll be in touch. Will you be visiting your aunt here much longer?"

"Another week or so," she said coolly. "Though I'd be tempted to stay six months to hear you explain all this."

Her mind was clicking away like mad, rejecting one possible explanation after the other. I could read it in her eyes and I had to laugh. "You're a very unusual dish, Lisa Huffmann," I said. "You're not like any *fräulein* I've ever met."

"And you're not like any man I've ever met," she said.

I smiled and turned to go. I took two steps, then turned back suddenly, reached out and pulled her to me. I kissed her and her lips remained unmoving, soft and wet, but unresponsive. Then, suddenly, they parted just enough to hint at what might be there.

"I didn't want you to forget," I said, pulling away. Her eyes were cool and taunting.

"I hardly think that would be possible," she said. "Even without that last item. You did come on rather strong."

This time I walked away; I grinned, looking back

at her from the sidewalk. And this time she waved, a small, contained wave, hardly more than the flick of her hand. I felt better as I walked down Kaiserlautern Strasse, in the same way one feels better after having discharged a debt. It always bothered me when I had to involve the innocent in this dirty game. It was often necessary, but I'd never got over being bothered by it. It was an old-fashioned, outmoded way of looking at things, I knew. Hawk himself often argued the point with me. "There are no innocents any longer," he'd say. "Everybody's involved today. Some are aware of it, most don't realize it, but they're still involved." It was ironic in a way, because it was right here in Germany that Adolf Hitler spelled it out when he said there were no more civilians. Everybody was a form of soldier, from housewives to kids, from factory workers to front-line troops. It was a concept that the Russians and the Chinese Communists had eagerly embraced for their own purposes. It made moral decisions unnecessary. It was the kind of thinking that made it easy to blow up a boat full of people to get at one person. Hawk, of course, maintained that we had to look at it that way in order to understand the enemy and his actions.

My thoughts were on the Russians and the Chinese as I decided to walk to Helga's place and I wondered which of them might be backing Dreissig and his NSH Party. It really didn't figure to be the

Russians unless they were setting him up as a clever pretext for action on their own part. It could be. They were Machiavellian enough to do it that way. The Chinese were a more likely suspect. They had a whole battery of agents out to make life miserable for the Russians and for us. They operated on the old anarchistic theory that the more chaos the merrier. And of course, there was the possibility of a combine of old German industrialists backing Dreissig, out to unify and rebuild the Fatherland, still flaming with the old militaristic nationalism. That was the theory I leaned toward myself. Hell, there was more nationalism in the world today than ever before. For every one of the major powers who thought in some form of internationalism there were ten new countries all fired up with the spirit of nationalism. Why shouldn't it rub off on the Germans? Given German background and history, it was not only natural but made to order. It was strange how the two major facets of the German national character could be summed up in two kinds of music, the march and the waltz. They loved both with a passion and they responded to both with the same intensity. Since the last war, we had made the waltz the most popular expression of the German character and now Dreissig was coming along with marches once again. And if he played loud enough, they'd start to march again. It was that simple, that certain and that complex.

I had reached Helga's place and found it was a walk-up and she lived on the fourth floor. I decided to knock. The key had been a gesture more than anything else.

V

It seemed everybody was surprised to see me. The utter astonishment in Helga's eyes as she opened the door made Lisa's mild surprise pale into nothingness. But before I could say anything, Helga squealed in joy and grabbed me in a bear hug, her breasts pressing hard into my chest through the soft blouse she had on. When she stepped back, her eyes still held a tinge of wonder.

"You did give me a key, didn't you?" I said, a little testily, I'm afraid.

"Yes, but I never thought I'd see you again," she answered, pulling me into the apartment.

"Why not?" I grumbled.

"You Americans have a saying, love 'em and leave 'em, I think is the way it goes. I just never expected you'd come back, that's all."

"You underestimate yourself," I told her. "Besides, you shouldn't put so much stock in old sayings."

Lisa's blue eyes sparkled and she reached up and nuzzled her head against my shoulder.

"I'm glad you're back," she said. "Really, I am."

As she stayed close against me, I looked over her shoulder at the apartment. It was small and very ordinary, almost without character of any kind. It had a furnished flat look to it that surprised me.

"How long can you stay?" Helga asked, bringing my attention back to her round, full breasts lightly touching my shirt, her somewhat pouty lips.

"Just tonight," I said.

"Then we'll have to make the most of it," she answered and her eyes had turned that smoky blue again, as though an invisible film had come over them. Her hands on my arm dropped to my chest and began to rub up and down in slow, semicircular motions.

"I was just about to eat . . . bratwurst," she said softly. "I've enough for two. Then we can take care of the other hunger." She moved away and I followed her into a small kitchen and a round table. While we ate, she talked of her day at work and asked what I had done. I told her I'd spent the day seeing various business acquaintances. She served me a beer and then a quarter of a water glass of "schnapps." It was like having a kind of boilermaker and as I watched her down hers, I saw that the top buttons of the blouse had been undone. Her breasts, held down by an overworked brassiere, spilled out in exciting loveliness. Downing her drink, she got up and came over to me.

"I thought about last night all day," she said, standing with her breasts only inches from my face. She cupped my head in her hands and looked down at me. "You were something special," she went on. "No one else has ever been able to stay with me, ever."

I could believe that quite easily, I told myself. I reached up, unsnapped the bra and put one hand under her left breast, feeling the soft yet firm flesh. Helga moaned and pressed my hand up.

"I told myself it was a one-time thing I had to forget," she breathed. "But seeing you here now has brought every moment rushing back to me. I want you, again . . . as much as I can have in one night."

Once again I felt the overpowering, animal sensuality of this girl, that feeling of desires barely under control, of overwhelming inner needs. But this time I wanted to see if it would be different, if I would be making love to her without experiencing that feeling of being an object. I squeezed gently and Helga's hands were moving up and down my torso and her body quivered. She moved backwards, keeping her hands on me, her breast firmly pressed against my palm, guiding us toward a small bedroom. The light from the living room cast a yellow glow on the bed. Helga flung off her blouse and I felt her skirt fall at my feet. Her tongue darted into my mouth, a thing of wild sensations and feverish circles. Her terrible inner drive was there again, a desperation that swept all else before it. She made love, I found myself thinking, as though she was sure there would be no tomorrow. Ordinarily, that would be a sensation of wonderful abandon, but with Helga that abandon was missing. Only the desperation came through. It bothered me, but her hands reaching into my trousers bothered me more. The hell with the analysis, I told myself. I'd think more about it later.

I pushed gently against her and she fell back upon the bed. I stepped back, stripped quickly, watching to see if she were observing me. Her eyes were closed and her breasts heaved. I put Wilhelmina and Hugo inside the fold of my clothes and lay down beside her. As my hand caressed her inner being, she cried out, her eyes still closed, pressing herself down upon my fingers, her rounded, cream-white stomach moving convulsively. She turned and rolled onto me, straddling my body, letting her breasts hang like beautiful, ripe pears against my lips. I tasted their sweetness and she pressed down, softly moaning and gasping. She stretched out on top of me, feverish with desire. I rolled her over and came to her, not gently, now, but almost brutally, matching the wild movements and thrust of her body. Suddenly she stiffened and a half-scream rose up from her very inner being. She fell back and I held still, but she clutched at me instantly.

"Again, again," she cried. "Make me come again,

now." I stayed with her, and her eyes were closed as I brought her to new peaks again. She would toss her blonde head from side to side as she half-laughed, half-sobbed in a pleasure beyond her ability to completely absorb. With any other girl I'd ever known, I would have felt almost sadistic, but with Helga, I still couldn't shake the feeling that she and not I was causing it all to happen. I was there, in her, hearing her cries of pleasure at what I was doing, and yet I felt there was a point I'd never reached with her. Somehow, for all her moans of delight and pleas for more, there was a core of impersonality about it. I couldn't shake that weird feeling of being an object, as though her physical rapture was somehow entirely apart from Helga Ruten, the person. It was an incompleteness that rubbed off, that transmitted the unsatisfied feeling I could not shake. It was an object lesson that the physical is never complete without the emotional. Helga's inner drive was so great, however, that it almost filled the void. Almost. She heaved, her stomach muscles contracting, her arms clutched around my neck and then, once again, she cried out in a long, breathy half-scream and her body stiffened. This time when she fell back onto the bed she closed her eyes, and went into an almost instant sleep.

I lay beside her and slept, too. It was much later when I woke to see Helga returning from the kitchen, biting into an apple, her round, full figure outlined in the light from the adjoining room. She glowed with an other-world quality, Eve, eternal Eve, standing with apple in hand. She sat down on the bed beside me.

"Stay here tomorrow," she said. "I'll only go in half a day and come back."

"I can't," I answered.

"What do you have to do tomorrow?" she asked, a hint of a pout in her voice. I raised my leg so she would lean her back against it which she promptly did.

"I need to go into East Berlin tomorrow," I said. "Got any ideas how I can do it?"

"You want to go to East Berlin?" she questioned, biting into the apple. "Why?"

"I must see a man on business, very personal business. But I hear the Russians are being very strict about entering these days."

"Very," she said, snapping off another piece of the apple. "I could get you into East Berlin."

I did a good job of sounding impressed rather than too eager.

"My cousin drives a produce truck into East Berlin every day," she went on casually. "I could call him and tell him to take you instead of his helper. The Russians know he has a helper with him every day. He owes me some favors."

"That would be great, Helga," I said, and this time my enthusiasm was very real. It was an absolutely perfect setup. She got up and started for the living room.

"I'll call him," she said.

"At this hour," I exclaimed. "It's nearly four o'clock in the morning."

"Hugo gets up early," she answered, her round rear silhouetted against the light. I smiled at the name. I had a friend Hugo and I silently wagered my friend Hugo was thinner and deadlier than her cousin Hugo. It wasn't a wager I expected to lose.

"I've got to give him time to call off his helper," she said. I shrugged. It was her cousin. If she wanted to wake the poor guy up it was all right with me. I lay back, listening to her dialing and then the sound of her voice.

"Hello, is this Hugo?" she asked. "This is Helga . . . Helga Ruten. Yes, I'll wait." Hugo probably wanted to put on a robe. Central heating was still an uncommon thing in Germany. "Yes, Hugo," I heard her go on. "I'm fine, but I need a favor. I have a friend who wants to go into East Berlin tomorrow. Yes . . . that's right . . . he's here with me now. We've been talking about it. I told him you could take him in as the helper in your produce truck."

There was a prolonged silence as she listened. "It would be perfectly simple," I heard her cut in. "I told him you and your helper crossed into East Berlin every day. Yes . . . I'll have him look for the truck with Hugo Schmidt on it. Yes . . . good, I have it. He'll be there. Do you have it all clear? You just take him into East Berlin. He'll go on his own from there, understand? Thank you, Hugo. '*Wiedersehen.*"

The phone clicked and Helga was beside me. "You must promise that if you come back tomorrow you'll come straight here," she said, her eyes intense. I promised. It was an easy promise. I was feeling really grateful to her. "You are to meet Hugo a block from the Brandenburg Gate checkpoint. His truck will be marked Hugo Schmidt. Wear shirt and trousers or a work jacket if you have one. Ten o'clock tomorrow morning. You can arrange about getting back with Hugo. He comes back in the afternoon."

I pulled her down to me and rolled over onto her. Instantly, her legs moved apart. "Thanks, honey," I said. "You don't know what a great favor you've just done me. When I come back I'll make love to you like you've never been made love to before."

There was something in her eyes, a sudden contraction of the pupils and she slid out from under me.

"I'll sleep in the living room," she said. "The couch folds out into a bed." Her eyes were looking down across my body and her mouth was set, almost grim.

"It's too bad," she said.

"What is?"

"That you must go," she answered, turning on her heel and closing the door behind her. She was a strange creature, I told myself again. There was a churning inside her, some deep disturbance. It was as if she were two people, the sensuously driven one of wild physical desire and someone else, someone cold and distant whom I'd never gotten at all near. The few hours left for sleep gave me no more time to play psychiatric detective. I turned over and went to sleep.

I'd somehow expected Helga would wake me, but I woke to the loud buzzing of an alarm clock in the next room. I went to shut it off and found I was alone in the apartment. A note on the table simply said, "Have gone to work. Helga." It was curt, impersonal. I shaved and called Howie Prailler at once and told him of my luck. He was as pleased as I was, and he gave me the details I still had to know.

"Your man lives at 79 Warschau Strasse. His name is Klaus Jungmann. Your code address is simple." I listened intently as he went over the code and fixed it firmly in my mind. "I'll get word to Hawk about this," Howie concluded. "It'll make the old buzzard's morning for him."

I stowed my jacket in a small tote bag I picked up at a drugstore and hurried to a corner exactly one block from the square outside the Brandenburg Gate, wearing shirt and trousers with shirtsleeves rolled up. It wasn't the greatest transformation, but I could pass as a truckman's helper. I was standing there waiting, feeling grateful to Helga and wondering what made her tick when it was Lisa Huffman's cool, contained face that popped up suddenly in my mind like a refreshing breeze. I hadn't time to think why when I saw the black panel truck pull around the corner with the words HUGO SCHMIDT—PRODUCE stenciled on the sides. True Teutonic punctuality; it was exactly ten o'clock. As I approached the truck, Helga's cousin leaned over and pushed the door open for me. He was a middle-aged man with a gruff, lined face. He wore a peaked cap and blue denim work clothes.

"I appreciate this very much," I said as openers. Hugo Schmidt merely grunted and nodded. "That Helga," he said. "Always involved in something. I never ask questions. I mind my own business."

The traffic at the checkpoint had grown heavier and was now backed up a block or two. It was almost entirely commercial traffic and the Vopos, the East German *Volkspolizei,* checked each vehicle as it approached the gate. I saw the large sign facing us as we neared the gate.

"*Achtung! Sie verlassen jetzt West Berlin!*" I translated it in my mind. "Attention! You are now leaving West Berlin!" It has the same ring of finality, of ominousness in both languages. You felt as though you were entering another world, which was more true than it sounded. As Hugo Schmidt's truck approached the gate, he leaned out and waved at the Vopos. They waved back, raised the gate and we moved on through. It had all happened so smoothly and simply I almost laughed.

"The advantage of crossing every day," Schmidt

said grimly. He drove on till he was beyond sight of the gate and then pulled to the curb.

"Where will I meet you to get back?" I asked. The blank look in his eyes revealed that it was a point he hadn't even thought about.

"I go back at four o'clock," he finally said. "Meet me at this corner at four."

"I'll be here," I waved. "And thanks again."

I watched the truck roll off and then cut across to the main thoroughfare of the Unter den Linden. The once-magnificent thoroughfare was shabby and dismal, with huge piles of rubble still standing about after all these years. I saw that the entire East section of Berlin wore a mantle of sordidness. I thought of a grand lady who now appeared only in shoddy, worn clothes. Compared to the sparkling vitality of West Berlin, it was a contrast that was as saddening as it was vivid. I hailed a cab and directed him to Warschau Strasse, one of the many streets in East Berlin the Russians had renamed. I got out as we reached the street and walked along the rows of dingy gray tenements that would have fitted comfortably into any slum in the States. I found number 79 and the name Klaus Jungmann on a ground-floor door. A small sign beneath the name said: Photo-Retouching.

I rang the bell and waited. I could hear shuffling around inside. Hawk had said that Jungmann was a "sleeper," an agent who is often left unused and dormant for years, contacted only for certain purposes.

Unlike international operatives such as myself, sleepers were valuable because of their complete anonymity. When the door finally opened I saw a tall, thin, sad-faced man with deep, brown eyes. He wore a faded blue smock and held a thin retouching brush in one hand. Beyond him, I took in a room cluttered with lamps, drawing table, paint cans and books. To one side I saw an air-brush motor.

"Yes?" Klaus Jungmann said. "May I help you?"

"I think so," I answered. "You are Klaus Jungmann, I take it."

He nodded, wariness creeping into the deep eyes.

"I want a photo of a very important man retouched," I said, going into the code Howie Prailler had given me. "His name is Dreissig. You have heard of him?"

"Heinrich Dreissig?" Jungmann asked cautiously.

"Dreissig, Dreissig, Dreissig," I said. "Three times stranger than anyone else."

Klaus Jungmann sighed and his shoulders lowered. He half-sat down on a high stool before the drawing table.

"Who are you?" he asked. When I told him his eyes widened. "I'm honored," he said sincerely. "But your coming here can only mean that something happened to Dennison."

"They got to him before I did," I replied. "Do you know what he was to pass on to me?"

Jungmann was nodding when we heard the sound of a car breaking to a screeching halt, followed by another and still another. There was the thump of car doors being slammed and feet pounding on pavement. Jungmann's eyes were wide, fastened on me. I shrugged and bolted for the window. Peering around the drawn shade, I saw two men in suits, one with a Tommy gun in hand, moving toward the entrance.

"Son of a bitch!" I exploded. "How the hell do they do it? Goddamn but they must be psychic!" The men weren't uniformed vopos. They were plainly some of Dreissig's boys and I interrupted swearing at the inexplicability of it to shout at Jungmann.

"Is there another way out of here?" I yelled.

"In the back, the rear door." I flung open the door, looked back to make sure he was following me, and raced down a long hallway to the rear of the tenement. The back door opened just as I neared it. There were two of them, each with an automatic rifle. I hit the floor, pulling Jungmann down with me as they opened fire. Wilhelmina was in my hand instantly and I let fly. I saw one double up as the big 9mm slug tore into him. The other one dived backwards out the door, but I knew he'd be waiting outside to blast us as we came out. I turned and started back down the long hallway.

"The roof," I called to Jungmann who was on my heels. We were almost at the staircase, just opposite Jungmann's apartment, when the two with the Tommy gun burst into the entranceway, spraying shots wildly. I dived sideways, back into the apartment, knocking Jungmann in ahead of me. I kicked the door shut with my foot and heard the automatic lock snap. They'd blast it open in a few seconds, but a few seconds could mean a lot. I spun around as I heard the smash of glass, saw the black snout of the automatic rifle poking through the ground-floor window. I yelled at Jungmann to hit the floor, but he hesitated, wide-eyed. The rifle chattered, spraying its deadly message in a wide arc. I saw Jungmann shudder, spin around, one hand clutching his throat where a shower of red burst forth. As he sank to the floor, I pegged a shot through the window, aiming just over and to the right of the rifle barrel. I heard the gasp of pain, heard the sound of the rifle clatter to the pavement. A burst of lead splintered the lock on the door, but I was ready and waiting as they burst in. I got off two shots that sounded like one. They pitched forward together to lay face down in the room. I waited a moment, listening, but there was no sound. There was still one of them waiting outside the rear door, I knew. I hadn't forgotten about him but I also knew the shooting would bring the vopos in a hurry. It had been fast, furious and noisy. By now there were probably 50 calls to the East German police.

I went over to Jungmann. His throat had been shot out, but he was still alive. Barely, but still living. I took a towel from the back of a chair and pressed it against his throat, watching it start to turn red instantly. Talking was out of the question for him, but his eyes were open and he might have the strength to nod. I leaned close to him.

"Can you hear me, Klaus?" I asked. His eyes blinked in answer.

"Who's supplying Dreissig with the money?" I questioned. "Is it the Russians?"

His head moved ever so slightly from left to right, a motion you could barely catch, but it had answered no.

"The Chinese. . . . Are they backing him?"

Once again the faint negative movement of the head came across. The towel was almost all red now. Time and Klaus Jungmann's life were running out together.

"Somebody in Germany?" I asked anxiously. "A combine of wealthy nationalists? An old military clique?"

Again his eyes answered no. I moved back as I saw his arm start to raise, waveringly. He gestured with one finger to a corner of the room where a fire pail filled with sand rested on the floor. I followed the flick of the finger again. He was definitely gesturing to the fire pail. I frowned.

"The fire pail?" I asked. The man nodded and as he did, his eyes came together and his head fell to one side. There would be no more questions to answer for Klaus Jungmann. I heard the sound of sirens approaching. It was time to make tracks. I went out the door, stepping over the two men. They were big, German types, blondish and square bodies. Bastards, I growled. They seemed to have eyes and ears everywhere.

I raced to the roof, pushed open the tin door that led to the rooftop and heard the sirens come to a halt below. I could hear more on the way. Like rooftops everywhere, it was tar and cinders with gutter drains edging the sides. I peered down over the back and saw the man starting to hurry from the rear door, tossing the rifle away. It was perhaps a foolish gesture, but I had to do it. The bastards had done nothing but bird-dog me in a way I'd never been bird-dogged before. I just wasn't going to let him get away. It only took one shot. I watched him stumble and fall forward, twitch for a moment and then lie still. The Vopos would react to the shot at once, I knew, but I was already racing across the adjoining rooftops until I had put about a dozen buildings between us. Then I stopped, slipped through one of the rooftop exit doors and went down the stairs to the street. It was a technique that had worked for uncounted hoodlums on the rooftops of New York, and now it worked for me in East Berlin. As I calmly sauntered down the street I glanced back at the activity and gathering crowds down the street. I walked to a little park not far away and sat down. I had some waiting time and I wanted to try and unravel what Klaus Jungmann had been trying to tell me.

The little bench was a small oasis of calm and

peace, I let my body relax in the Yoga method of bringing about heightened mental powers through complete physical relaxation. The fire pail full of sand had me going in circles. Jungmann had said no to the Russians, the Chinese and to homegrown backers. Yet Dreissig wasn't getting money out of sand. That didn't make sense. Maybe from someone who dealt in sand? That didn't make much more sense either, but it was a possibility. It would fit in with the German industrialist theory. But then Jungmann had knocked that down. A sixth sense told me I was going up the wrong alley. I started over again.

A fire pail filled with sand. Maybe I was hung up on the wrong thing? Was it the fire pail or the sand that was the clue? I tried the fire pail angle and came up with absolutely nothing. I had to stick with the sand, but what the hell had he meant by it? I went over it again step by step. I rested my head back over the top of the bench and let my mind drift into that twilight zone of free association. Dreissig and sand . . . he was getting money from soneone with sand . . . someone or something or someplace. A light suddenly flashed and began to glow. Not someone with sand, but *someplace* with sand. The light burned brighter. Sand . . . the desert . . . the Arab countries. Of course, I exclaimed aloud, sitting bolt upright. The oil-rich Arabs, that's what Jungmann had been trying to get across . . . sand and the Arabs. It was all suddenly dangerously clear and logical. All it would take was one wealthy

Arab chieftan or big wheel. Maybe Dreissig had hatched the plan and sold his benefactors on it, whatever it was. I was more than certain that it had to be a two-way street. They were supplying him with money to further his plans and those plans had to include something big for the Middle East. Whatever it was, I knew it wouldn't be aimed at bringing peace and calm to the explosive area of the Middle East. You could damn well count on that much. I had the distinctly uneasy feeling that if Dreissig wasn't stopped in the early stages of whatever he was planning, he wouldn't be stopped at all. There comes a time when events and movements gather a momentum that only a collision can halt.

I didn't need to hear Hawk's words. I knew what they'd be: Get in there and find out what they're up to. The first step in that was to get back to West Berlin. The second was still up for grabs. I leaned toward the idea of a meeting with Dreissig himself. I could pose as an admirer, a wealthy American admirer. Perhaps I could get into his confidence. I'd check it out with Hawk, but the idea had its appeal.

I got up and started to walk back to where I was to meet Hugo Schmidt. Dreissig's operation was neither small-time nor amateur any longer. The way his boys kept nailing me wherever I went was sure proof of that. They certainly were the cleverest bunch I'd run into in many a year, or they were just plain lucky. Maybe it was a combination of the two. I paused to pick up a newspaper and, leaning against a lamppost, I waited for the little panel truck to appear.

The afternoon traffic back into West Berlin was growing heavier. Hugo Schmidt was not as punctual as he'd been this morning. Four o'clock came and went. At four-thirty I folded the newspaper and stood waiting. At five o'clock I tossed the paper away and began pacing back and forth, anxiously scanning every panel truck that turned the corner. At six o'clock I felt a cold hand gripping my chest. The truck hadn't even come by. It hadn't appeared because there was no reason for it to appear. I wasn't expected here at four o'clock. I wasn't expected to be here at all, at any time. I was supposed to be dead with Klaus Jungmann.

It was a chilling thought, but an undeniably clear one. Suddenly a helluva lot of bits and pieces were fitting together to explain a number of previously unrelated things. Dreissig's bully-boys, for example. They were neither omnipotent nor extra efficient. I had been fingered for them right from the start, and the finger belonged to one Helga Ruten. Eager, earthy, blonde Helga. She was the only one who knew I was entering East Berlin this morning and where, when and how. She had set it all up for me, only it wasn't for me. And yesterday, when they tried to tail me to AXE headquarters, Helga was the only one who knew I'd arrived in the city. Obviously, she had phoned from the castle and had them set and waiting when I drove her up to her place. It was no wonder they latched onto me with such ease. And today they had waited for me to contact Jungmann, then moved in to kill two birds with one stone. But this bird was very much alive and very angry. Mad as hell, in fact.

It was so goddamned obvious now, that I felt like kicking myself. It also explained the look of shocked astonishment on her face when I appeared at her place last night. They had no doubt phoned her and told her I'd been done in by the Berlin-Hamburg Express. The call to her cousin, Schmidt, had been a call to Dreissig's men, of course, setting me up right in front of me. That took nerve and a kind of insolence I was determined to pay back. But one thing, one big fat thought, kept intruding on my conclusions. Helga and the Rhine boat explosion; it didn't fit in right. If she were one of Dreissig's crew how did it happen that she was aboard the boat and almost killed in the explosion. There was no faking about that bit when I pulled her out of the Rhine. She'd had it. Her near-shock and the torrent of tears afterward were the real thing, as real as those hours in bed with me. I could probably come up with an explanation for that reality, but the excursion boat was a jarring note. The only way to get at the absolute truth was to get at Helga. She could be a good start at Dreissig, too, if she were what I thought.

I walked to where I could see the tall, gray concrete wall. It was not only forbidding enough, but the Russians had decorated it with electrified wire and barbed wire. It ran in an unbroken line in either direction, truly, as the Berliners had come to call it, a concrete curtain.

Nick Carter, I told myself, you have a problem.

VI

Darkness covered East Berlin, and the headlights of vehicles lined up at the crossing mingled in with the bright floodlights illuminating the square. I walked along the Berlin wall and contemplated trying to scale it despite the barbed and electrified wire. I saw a couple of spots where I felt I could pick my way around the wire. That idea went up in smoke when I saw the floodlights go on as night fell. They illuminated the entire lower half of the wall. Anyone trying to scale it would be as conspicuous as a horsefly on an ice cream cone. I even walked over to where the river Spree ambled its way from East Berlin into West Berlin. It was a possibility, but a slim one. The Vopos were patrolling the sector by the wall with very large and efficient German shepherds. They also floodlighted that section of the river so anyone swimming across wouldn't have the advantage of the dark and the water.

I returned to a corner near the large square and watched the vehicles queue up, recalling how I had heard that the Russians and the East German police had gone to great lengths to halt the steady stream of fugitives fleeing the glories of the peoples' democracy. They had indeed done a thorough job, I'd found out. Getting back to Helga was rapidly becoming a major problem, one I hadn't figured on. I could come to one conclusion from what I saw. The only way out was the same way everyone else was taking, through the checkpoint and the gate. It was a short enough distance and with any luck I could run it. But first I had to find a vehicle.

The streets of East Berlin, I quickly learned, grow deserted soon after dark falls. Night life is confined to Stalinallee off to the east and even that is tame. There were few people and fewer cars except for those on their way to the checkpoint. Finally I spotted one, a small Mini-Cooper standing outside an all-night diner. It had been converted into a plumber's utility vehicle with the top rack carrying an assortment of toolbags, acetylene torches and short pieces of pipe. The one word, "*Klempner,*" was lettered across the door. The plumber, I saw peering through the diner window, was just finishing a cup of coffee. I stayed in the shadows till he came out. He was opening the car door when I came up behind him. This had to be fast and noiseless. He tried to whirl as I clamped an arm around his neck. I applied the pressure quickly, just enough, and felt him go limp. It was a dangerous hold, fatal if the least little bit too much pressure was applied. He'd be all right and awake in fifteen minutes or so. I dragged him into a hallway and gave him a pat on the cheek.

"Sorry, pal," I murmured. "It's all in a good cause, though. You won't know it, but you'll be one of those unsung heroes."

The Mini-Cooper was hardly a very reassuring vehicle to use for gate-crashing. I felt as though I were on a tricycle as I drove the little car up and down the streets, watching for a break in the line waiting at the gate. I'd need a running start, with all the speed I could get out of this little chariot. I slowed down as two buses moved on through the checkpoint. It was open with no one on line. I turned, pressed the accelerator to the floor and headed straight for the wooden gate marking the east side of the Brandenburg Gate. There were a few unfortunate little details I hadn't counted on though. The first one was the fact that there had been so many past attempts to crash the gate that a special detail had been posted to watch for any vehicle speeding into the square.

As soon as I hit the edge of the square, alarm bells sounded and the raucous hoot of a klaxon screamed. Directly ahead of me I saw heavy, spiked steel bars rise up out of the pavement. Too late, I remembered that a number of enterprising Germans had crashed the gate using tanks and the Russians had special tank barriers installed to rip up the treads. The pointed, spiked steel bars would go through the Mini-Cooper like a bayonet through a straw man. I swerved as the first of the barriers loomed up in front of me. The little car went over on two wheels and I heard the tearing of metal as it scraped alongside the bars. I managed to keep her from going over and aimed at four Vopos who were on their knees, drawing a bead on me with their rifles. They leaped for safety as I barrelled into them.

I was running parallel to the wall now, and I heard the shots zonk into the rear fenders. They were aiming at the tires. I swerved again, heading back across the square toward one of the streets leading from it. As I reached it, I saw a big half-track pull out of the cross-street ahead of me and come to a halt, blocking off the street. The four Vopos in the half-track had leaped out the far side and were aiming their rifles at me from behind the truck, expecting I'd either ram myself against their heavy vehicle or sensibly come to a stop.

I decided against both. There was just enough scraping room between the end of the half-track and the building line. I swung the Mini-Cooper up onto the sidewalk and careered past them. I swung sharply and cut down another cross-street just as a *polizei* cruiser took up the chase, roaring after me with siren screaming. I knew I was playing a losing game if I stuck with the Mini-Cooper. I took the first corner on two wheels and braked to a halt just around the curve. I got out and started running. The pursuing police car did just what I'd figured it would do, careering around the corner to plow right into the Mini-Cooper. I heard the roar as both cars went up in flames. It would keep everybody busy for a little while.

I ran through the nearest building, cut back and mingled with the crowd that had gathered. More army jeeps and cars had come up, and I casually sauntered away. It had been a good try, but they don't pay off on good tries. I was still in East Berlin and that damned wall was looking even more unassailable.

I could see why an air of resignation and discouragement permeated the East Berliner's life. After the crowds dispersed, I holed up again in a doorway where I could watch the traffic line at the checkpoint. I was racking my brain and coming up with nothing, except that I didn't dare try the same stunt again. They were on full alert now and had put on added men. As the hours crept by I saw that it was mostly heavy-duty truck traffic that passed into West Berlin during the late hours. I was feeling more frustrated and it was nearing midnight when I saw the four big tractor-trailers pull up to the checkpoint. The last one extended back almost to where I was standing in the dark doorway. I watched the Vopos make a thorough check of each trailer, examining the driver's papers first and then having him open up the doors of each trailer. It was routine procedure but very thorough, and as I watched, the glimmer of an idea caught fire.

The small pair of wheels tucked up under the forward part of the trailer had caught my eye. A crossbar arrangement beneath a small axle supported the two wheels which were used only when the trailer was detached from its cab. I watched the Vopos walk back to their positions at the gate and heard the first of the four-truck convoy come to life. One by one the other engines thundered, and as the first tractor-trailer started to move through the exit gate, I was a dark figure, crouched over, racing for the last trailer in line. Diving underneath, I pulled myself up on the undercarriage wheels, using the cross-bars to cling to while I squeezed my legs in between the small axle and the underside of the trailer. Flattening myself up against the bottom of the trailer, I held my breath as the truck started to move. I could see the uniformed legs of the Vopos go by as we gathered speed, then the black-and-white stripes on the gates. We were across, in West Berlin. I clung to my precarious position until the truck finally halted for a light. Slipping my legs out, I dropped to the ground and rolled from under the trailer as the huge wheels started to roll again. My legs were somewhat cramped, but they worked themselves out quickly as I hurried along the night streets.

Unlike the drab and dreary atmosphere of the Eastern sector, West Berlin was alive and bright and

I quickly got a taxi. On the way to Helga's place, I used the time to reload Wilhelmina and secured the Luger back in the shoulder holster under my shirt. The key Helga had given me was in my pocket. It would be used this time.

A sliver of light creeping out from under the door told me that Helga was still up. I opened the door with one quick motion. She was in the bedroom, the door open, and she whirled as she heard me enter. I didn't need to say anything. Her eyes widened and she stood there transfixed, wearing a dark skirt and a light-green sleeveless blouse. Her spell of astonishment shattered as she suddenly made a dive for the tall dresser that stood against the bedroom wall. She yanked open the top drawer and reached inside. She almost had the gun out when I slammed the drawer shut on her wrist. She cried out in pain. I grabbed her arm, twisted and pulled open the drawer. Her fingers opened and the gun dropped back into the drawer. I slammed it shut and flung Helga onto the bed. A small overnight bag she had been packing was knocked to the floor. She was still bouncing on the bed as I grabbed a shock of her blonde hair and yanked her head around. She gasped in pain and wrapped her arms around my waist, partially raising herself on one knee.

"Please don't hurt me," she emplored. "I . . . I'm glad you're alive. Really, I am."

"Of course," I said. "You're ecstatic over it. I could

tell that by the way you went for the gun. It was a touching gesture."

"I was afraid you were going to hurt me," she said. "You . . . you looked so angry."

"You don't have to wonder about it," I told her. "You can be sure of it unless you give me some fast answers."

I kicked at the overnight bag spilled on the floor. "You were going to meet your friends, weren't you?" I said, in what was more of a statement than a question. "Maybe you were going to meet Dreissig."

"I was going to the country," she said, still clinging to my waist. "I'm really not one of them." Her eyes were round and pleading. "I got into helping them because I needed the money."

"Try again," I snapped. "That one isn't selling. I know Dreissig is being financed by Arab money. You're going to fill me in on the details. Who is it that's backing him?"

"I don't know anything," she repeated. "You've got to believe me.'"

"Sure, and then get my head examined."

"You don't understand," she began, but I cut her off.

"You're right," I said. "I don't understand a lot of things, but you're going to make them all clear to me. I don't understand a girl who can make love to a man, get out of bed and set him up for death. I don't understand about you being on the Rhine boat either."

"I can explain all those things," she said quickly.

"Good, but do it later. First you're going to tell me what you know about Dreissig."

She was starting to run her hand up my leg. "I don't know anything, I tell you," she said.

I snapped her head back hard and she gasped in pain. "Let's start over," I rasped. "How does Dreissig get the money and where is it banked?"

She must have read the message in my eyes, the message that said I wasn't kidding and I wasn't going to be bothered by squeamishness. In turn, the sudden contraction of her pupils, the cold pinpoints that flared in her eyes, warned me. Out of the corner of her eye I saw her hand come around, fist clenched, in a short, flat, upward arc and I knew immediately where she was aiming. I managed to twist my hip and take the blow on the hard muscle of my thigh. I backhanded her and heard her teeth rattle as she flipped off the far side of the bed and hit the floor. I reached across the bed and pulled her up by the hair. I pushed her face down into the pillow and pressed one hand down on a spot just at the top of the spinal cord. Even muffled against the pillow, her scream was bloodcurdling. I pulled her around and she screamed again. Her pretty face was contorted in pain and the left side of her body was twisted in agony. I raised a hand and she fell back, cowering.

"No, God, no," she gasped out. "My left side . . . it hurts so. I can't feel anything but pain."

It would pain her for some while that way, I knew. I didn't like doing this any better than she liked being on the receiving end. But I kept thinking that that boatload of people didn't like being blown to bits either. I grabbed her by the neck, my hand big enough to completely encircle it, and squeezed. Her hands clutched helplessly at mine.

"Dreissig, Helga," I said. "Who's backing him?"

"Ben Mussaf," she gasped. I relaxed my grip and let her fall back on the bed. Ben Mussaf, Sheik Abdul Ben Mussaf. He was one of the desert tycoons who had long objected to Nasser's prominence in Arab affairs. He had billions from oil, good contacts with the other desert sheiks and apparently ambitions of his own. It was a neat combine.

"How does he send the money and where?" I asked Helga's pain-wracked form. She hesitated. I reached out and it had an instantaneous effect.

"Gold," she blurted out at once.

A whistle escaped me. But it figured. Gold, the most stable of all currencies. Dreissig could trade it on the open market as he saw fit, or exchange it for marks, dollars, francs or whatever he needed. It eliminated the need for large, attention-getting deposits in local banks, too. It was good anywhere, any time, in any market. But it had one problem. Sizeable gold shipments couldn't be stored in a piggybank.

"Where is the gold kept?" I questioned Helga. She

rose up on one elbow and her arms in the sleeveless blouse were shaking with both pain and fright.

"I . . . I'll tell you," she said, looking into the cold centers of my eyes. "Just let me have a cigarette first. Please, just one."

I nodded. She knew I meant business. A cigarette might calm her down further and make her realize she'd better cooperate fully. On the end table with the one lamp was a heavy glass ash tray and a pack of cigarettes. Helga reached back to pick up the cigarettes and the ash tray. Her back was to me for a moment as she leaned over to move the ash tray. Thanks to the sleeveless blouse, I saw her shoulder muscle contract and I reacted instantly. Otherwise I'd have had my head split wide open as, with cat-like speed, Helga flung the heavy ash tray at me. I managed to make the blow a glancing one that bounced off the side of my skull. As it was, I saw pinwheels and rockets exploding, and I heard rather than saw Helga's figure rushing past me. I reached out for her wildly, as I shook my head to clear it. She dodged my hand with ease, and when I turned she stood against the dresser, the revolver in her hand.

"Pig!" she spat out. "You'll be sorry for this. You want explanations? I'll give them to you. They'll be the last ones you will hear. You want to know about the Rhine boat? I'll tell you about it. I set the bomb. That's right, I set it. Only the *verdammte* thing went off thirty seconds too soon. I'd have been killed along with the others if I hadn't been climbing over the stern rail to dive overboard. It blew me free."

I watched the blue steel that were her eyes. I'd seen her jaw set grimy before, but never the impassive coldness she exuded. I remembered the thirsting, feverishly eager creature that remained curiously impersonal while making wild love. She was two people indeed, and one of them was a callous, cold-hearted, complete bitch.

"Does that satisfy you about the Rhine boat?" she went on. I nodded and held her eyes with my gaze.

"You want to know where the gold is kept?" she added. "Ben Mussaf is coming for a planning session tomorrow night. He's bringing a large shipment. Too bad you won't be around to find out."

She was still screaming at me and I kept my eyes riveted on her. I had nothing to lose now, and I was playing for time. There was another Helga, I knew, the one who wanted me with such fierce desire she couldn't help herself. If I could evoke even a little piece of that one, just long enough, I might have a chance. I'd noticed that the cord from the bedside lamp ran to a socket in the baseboard of the wall not far from where I stood.

"You were going to explain something else to me," I said, shifting minutely to the right. "About going to bed with me. I don't believe that was an act, you see."

The gun stayed steadily on me, but her eyes softened for an instant. "It wasn't an act," she said. "I found out who you were that first evening at the castle. I listened on the extension to your long-distance call. But you're a very compelling man. You reached something in me."

"And last night?" I asked, moving imperceptibly again. "You can't tell me you've forgotten already. I won't believe you."

"I haven't forgotten," she said. "It is just done with, that's all."

"It was good, though, wasn't it, Helga?" I grinned at her. My foot was now inches from the cord and the plug in the wall socket. "Want to go to bed with me again, Helga? . . . Right now? Remember my mouth on your breasts? Remember how you went through the roof when I came to you?"

Helga's breasts were rising and falling with deep, rapid breaths. "You bastard!" she said through clenched teeth. I heard the click of the hammer as she tightened on the trigger. I lifted the toe of my shoe and yanked. The light went out and I dropped to one side as the shot whistled over my head. I brought my arm around in a wide arc, catching Helga at the knees, toppling her backwards as a second shot went into the ceiling. I was atop her instantly, diving for the gun. She outfoxed me by letting go of it and I went sprawling, gun in hand, while she rolled over and raced out of the room. I saw her disappear out of the living room and into the outside hallway. Tossing the gun aside, I went after her, hearing her take the stairs two at a time, heading for the roof. I almost caught her at the top of the stairs, but she managed to slam the roof door and I had to pull back to avoid a bashed face.

The roof was dark, but I spotted her a few feet from the far edge. The nearest building was a good six to eight feet away.

"Don't!" I yelled. "You'll never make it." She ignored me, took a running start and jumped. I grimaced as she caught the opposite roof with her arms, clawed at the edge for a moment and then fell backwards, a long death-scream splitting the night. I turned away. I wanted to feel sorry for her, but it just wasn't there. I was really sorry about only one thing, the large chunk of information I hadn't gotten out of her. I was suddenly very tired. It had been a rugged day. I hurried down the stairs and out into the night. A second-rate hotel not far away was happy to rent me a room, and I was grateful for any quiet place to sleep.

I closed my eyes knowing that in the morning I had to figure out where Abdul Ben Mussaf was meeting Dreissig. It was a summit conference I desperately wanted to attend. I had the sober and unshakable feeling that the sacrifices of yesterday and the hopes of tomorrow depended on it.

VII

I'd found a coffee shop open early, and I was trying to sort out the jumble of thoughts whizzing around my head over a hot, strong cup of *Deutsche kaffee*. Despite her protestations to me, it was clear that Helga had been an important member of Dreissig's team, the group I once had thought so uncannily efficient. Now that I knew the picture, they'd actually been rather bumbling as I looked back on it. I enjoyed knowing that by now, having no doubt learned what had happened to their Helga, they'd be more than a little nervous and probably very aware of who they were dealing with. They'd had three cracks at me, besides trapping me in East Berlin, and all they really had for it was at least six of their boys dead plus Helga. And I was still around. They deserved to be nervous.

I also realized something else. For all my preoccupation with this man, Dreissig, I'd never even seen a picture of him, and I wondered what he was like. Tall, short, calm, high-strung? Was he good in the clinches or the kind that would come apart? Those things were important. They could make a lot of difference in knowing what to expect and what was needed. I really only knew one thing about him. He had big plans and big ambitions, all of which I had yet to find out about. Helga's remark about Abdul Ben Mussaf kept whirling around. He was due tonight with a major shipment of gold and Helga had been packing to attend the meeting. An overnight bag only. That said something. Where she was headed was near enough, yet far enough.

She had employed a technique of building fiction on fact. There had been a produce truck to drive me into East Berlin, but Cousin Hugo was a phony. There had been a castle in which she knew her way around, but, I was betting, her "uncle" was a phony, too. Uncle was Dreissig, I was willing to wager. What better place to hold secret meetings than an old castle? What better place to stash away gold than an old castle? It was a natural and I recalled the tightly closed doors on the left side as she showed me around. Of course, that was it, the old *schloss* overlooking the Rhine. She had even picked the spot near it to explode the excursion boat so she could go there and dry out.

I calculated rapidly. Figuring on crossing the *Autobahn*, delays at the various checkpoints and the mileage to the middle Rhineland, it would be at least a four-hour drive. I needed a good, fast car, and I didn't want to go near one of the rental places. They could be clever enough to watch them, figuring I might try to get a car for myself. But I knew where I could get one. I only hoped she had replaced the other one by now. I couldn't help chuckling as I left the *kaffeehaus.* I could see Lisa Huffmann's face already.

She opened the door wearing a clinging jersey blouse of an iridescent red with blue-on-blue checked slacks, very tailored and very form fitting. The up-turned curve of her breasts were hard not to watch, but I kept my eyes on her face, saw the raised-eyebrow wariness in her eyes, the faint smile of amusement that played around her finely molded lips.

"You do turn up at the most unexpected times," she said.

"A habit," I smiled. "How's the new car? Did you get it yet?"

"Something tells me I should say no," she answered, her eyes growing more wary. "But the answer is yes. Last night, in fact. Same as the other only cream."

"Good," I said, unable to avoid feeling apologetic. "I'd like to borrow it."

Incredulousness now nudged itself alongside the bemused wariness in her eyes.

"You've got to be kidding," she said finally.

"I was never more serious," I said, breaking into a

wide and uncontrollable grin. The ridiculously funny aspects of the whole thing were too much for my normally off-beat sense of humour. Lisa Huffmann looked at me and then began to laugh and in seconds we both stood there howling.

"You're too much, really," she got in between laughs. "Did you bring your checkbook?"

"I won't need it this time," I said, pulling myself together. "Honest, I won't."

"No railroad trains?" she said with mock gravity.

"No railroad trains," I echoed.

"Nobody shooting at us?"

"Nobody shooting at us."

"You know, that was a very expensive ride you took last time," she said seriously. "Wouldn't it be cheaper for you just to rent a car?"

I started to answer, but she cut me off. "I know," she said. "You can't answer that now."

"You're learning," I grinned. A sudden thought flashed. I really only needed the Mercedes to get there. I'd be on my own after that, facing countless unknown contingencies.

"Why don't you come with me?" I said. "When we get where I'm going I'll leave you and you can turn around and drive the car right back. You'll know that everything is back in good condition."

She thought it over for a minute. "The idea appeals to me," she said. "Aunt Anna does want to go shopping sometime tomorrow."

"Good," I said. "Then you'll know you'll have your new car back and ready to go."

She disappeared into the apartment and came back with a small purse and her keys. We picked up the Mercedes 250SL at a small private garage around the corner and took off. I was happy at my brainstorm. There was a fresh, irreverent quality to Lisa that would make the trip infinitely more pleasant than driving out alone. Never knowing what lay ahead, I'd long ago developed the philosophy of enjoying things while you can. It would be a dull, boring trip. Why not a lovely girl to make it pleasanter. And she was lovely. Later, as we tooled along the *Autobahn*, she was a warm and witty conversationalist, intellectually stimulating and physically rewarding.The slacks didn't conceal the long, lovely shape of her thighs and her waist was small. She wasn't all that full-busted, but there was a pert, upturned curve to her breasts that matched the saucy tilt of her chin. Her eyes, really more light brown than hazel, I decided, were quick to laugh and the cool, contained composure really reflected a helluva well balanced attitude toward life.

"Where did you learn your English?" I asked her.

"In school," she answered promptly.

"You must have had a great course," I commented.

"I did," she replied. "And don't forget all those American movies."

I was sorry when we reached the verdant banks of

the Rhine. There had been an unusually long series of delays at every checkpoint, both east and west, and traffic on the *Autobahn* had been terribly heavy. It was late afternoon before we were rolling alongside the river. She had tried to draw me out during the drive, but I had turned her aside. But once again I was aware of the cool speculation with which she studied me.

"Did you decide between the avenging angel and the super jewel thief?" I grinned at her.

"In a way," she said. "I think you're a little of both wrapped up in something else. How's that for openers, Nick Carter?"

I had to laugh. She was damned good with those very American expressions. And it wasn't a bad description at that. My eyes were searching the mountains, scanning the tops of the towering castles that rose up from the hills. I didn't want to miss it, approaching from a different direction as we were. Then I glimpsed it, looming up ahead, and I turned off the road onto the smaller secondary road. I slowed down and found the little lane that led up to the castle. I nosed into it so that Lisa could back out. I didn't want to take her any further.

I was turning to her to say goodby when three men appeared out of the bushes and approached the car. They wore white shirts and gray trousers tucked into army boots. A shield with crossed swords was sewn onto the breast pocket of each shirt. It wasn't exactly a uniform, but then it wasn't exactly civilian dress either. It fitted Dreissig's political technique of treading a neat line, of saying something without saying it.

"This is a private road," one of them said politely, but firmly. They were fairly young, cold-eyed, husky.

"I'm sorry, I didn't know," I apologized, backing out onto the road. My trained glance had spotted two more of the shield-emblazoned white shirts peering out from the trees. "Uncle" Dreissig was here, all right. The quiet old *schloss* had become a beehive of activity. I drove down the road, pulled over on the other side of a curve, out of sight of the castle guards.

"Thanks, sweetie," I said, sliding out. "This is where I get off. See, I told you it would be a nice, pleasant ride. Take good care of yourself and the car. I might need it again sometime."

She had slid behind the wheel and was looking deep into my eyes. "What are you going to do here?" she asked directly, unsmiling, concern in her soft-brown orbs.

"It's still not quiz time," I said gently. "Go on home. And thanks again."

This time it was my turn to be surprised. She leaned out the window, and her lips were soft and yielding. It was an almost tender kiss, sweet as honey.

"Be careful," she said seriously. "I've gotten fond of you in a crazy way. I still want to know what you're going to do here all alone. It has something to do with that castle, hasn't it?"

I grinned at her and patted her cheek. "Go on home," I said. "I'll be in touch."

I walked back down the road, pausing to watch her drive off slowly. Then I cut into the bushes and proceeded carefully and quietly toward the little lane. The bushes expanded rapidly into fairly thick woods, and as I neared the lane I cut up and started climbing the hill, moving up through the trees paralleling the lane. From time to time I could hear voices and the sound of cars moving along the lane. As I remembered, the lane led right up to the front gate, but the bushes left off a hundred feet back. My memory was unfortunately too accurate. That's exactly what happened, leaving far too much open space to cross in daylight, especially with the white-shirted guards standing at the drawbridge and the gatehouse. I did notice one happy thing which had escaped me during my first visit to the castle. The moat was the moat in name only, nothing more than a wide, dry ditch surrounding the old castle.

I moved along the edge of the treeline to the rear of the castle. There was no activity back there and I decided to chance it. I raced from cover and scrambled down into the dry moat where I saw a kind of makeshift drawbridge of planks leading down to a pair of heavy, oaken doors. I climbed up on it and leaned against one of the doors. Surprisingly it moved, creaking and reluctant, but it moved. I slipped in, pushed it closed behind me and saw I was in the wine cellar once again. As I crawled between the rows of big, fat wine casks, a little cubbyhole in my brain opened up at once to remind me that something about the cellar had bothered me when I visited it with Helga. I gazed around and had the same feeling again. But whatever was bothering me still danced on the edge of my consciousness, part of that strange, mental mechanism that was at once irritating and beneficial. It would come to me, I knew. As I went up the stone steps and into the stone hallway, I heard much noise and activity in the direction of the kitchen and the main dining hall and the sounds of chairs being moved and tables being set.

I went in the other direction, up the wide stone steps to the second floor of the keep. Beyond the small, square alcove just off the steps, I saw the three rooms still tightly shut. Moving cautiously, checking carefully at each archway, I reached the first of the rooms. I was certain I'd find the gold, probably in bars, possibly in sacks. Maybe arms and ammunition, too. It turned out I was in the right church, but the wrong pew. It wasn't gold I found but feathers, feathers attached to real live birds in rows of huge cages—big birds of golden-brown with black markings. Long, vicious talons and sharp, piercing eyes, fierce, proud heads and the soft gold of the golden eagle, perhaps the fiercest, fastest of the falcon family. Each bird was in its own cage, some hooded, some unhooded, each a fierce, winged killer.

I slipped out and in the other two rooms found more of the eagles, plus a lot of falconry equipment, jesses, bewits, leashes, rufter hoods and the like. I went back to the first room and looked at the fierce-eyed birds. Most were fully adult eagles and most had a little bait left at the bottom of their spacious cages. Herr Dreissig was obviously a devotee of the ancient sport of kings, falconry. But these were not peregrines or kestrels, but the far more powerful, far larger golden eagles. Obviously he had been developing a variation on the ordinary falconry. At sometime I had heard that the golden eagle had been trained to hunt in the same manner as the falcon. This hobby no doubt added to his rapport with the Arab sheiks, but it was a jarring and entirely unexpected note here in the middle of the Rhineland.

As I moved across the room, I saw one of the great eagles watching me with unusual interest. I'd seen falcons in action, seen what their talons could do to flesh and bone. These huge eagles, deadliness and beauty combined, could tear a man to bits and the iciness in their unfeeling eyes gave me a chill. I closed the door quietly and stood in the hallway, thinking of where to look next. My first guess had been a big fat zero. I didn't have long to think, for footsteps were echoing on the stones, coming my way. I squeezed into a small space behind the arch of the corridor entrance. I could peer through a wide space between two of the stones and found myself facing a suit of armor on a stand across the alcove. One of Dreissig's men appeared with a robed Arab wearing the traditional burnoose. The guard spoke to him in English.

"Herr Dreissig asks that Ben Kemat, most honored advance representative for His Excellency Abdul Ben Mussaf, please wait here. He will be with you in moments."

The Arab bowed his head and the guard clicked his heels and disappeared down the hallway. The Arab was rather light complexioned with a pair of harsh, deep eyes. What with his robes, burnoose and headgear, most of him was covered up. Banking on the implications of the conversation I'd just overheard, that Dreissig and this character hadn't met, I decided to move boldly. I had a deep tan. Wearing the Arab's outfit I could get by among non-Arabs, at least. I wouldn't make it in a tent of sheiks, but here I had a better than even chance. If Ben Kemat were here to arrange things for the boss's arrival, it would be a made-to-order chance not only to get to Dreissig, but to draw him out. It might even be a golden opportunity to wrap the whole thing in one shot. I dropped Hugo into my hand, the pencil-thin blade of the stiletto cold against my palm. I never liked the sudden sneak attack, but I was dealing with a group of boys who had a patent on it. Besides, this had to be fast and permanent. It wouldn't do to have the real Ben Kemat wake up in the middle of my briefing. I moved out from behind the archway, flipped the blade hard and fast and watched the Arab stagger, then sink slowly to the floor. He lay there, looking like a big pile of rags.

I moved fast, putting on his outfit and then dragging him across the floor. I'd already figured a nice, safe place for him. I hadn't figured on how much work it is to get a body into a suit of armor. It took much too much time, and I was sweating profusely when I finished and closed the visor down on the suit of armor once again standing against the wall. I had reason to sweat for I'd just finished securing the damn thing to its stand when I heard footsteps and turned to see the tall man in the gray suit approaching. Cold-blue eyes, carefully waved gray-blond hair, a trim athletic frame. His face, too imperious to be handsome to me, had plenty of matinee-idol appeal to it nonetheless. He held out his hand and I was surprised to find he had an iron grip. He was probably a physical culture enthusiast, too. His smile was disarming, ingratiating and just a shade too mechanical. But of course, I was being critical. I knew he'd go over with plenty of socko on a speaker's platform.

"Welcome, Ben Kemat," Heinrich Dreissig said in excellent English. "I suspect you and I will follow the same procedure as His Excellency and I do?"

He saw the frown that crossed my face. "I mean we will speak in English," he explained. His Excellency's German is not that fluent and my Arabic is limited. But we both know English."

"Ah, please," I said with a half bow. "I would appreciate it." Dreissig led the way to the room which I'd glimpsed as an office. A large map of Israel and the surrounding Arab territories had been pulled down to almost fill half a wall. At Dreissig's gesture, I sat facing it. He was giving me a charming smile that didn't mask a calculating once-over.

"You do not look Arabian," he remarked casually.

"My father was English," I replied matching casualness. "My mother raised me in Arabia and gave me her name."

"The agenda for His Excellency's visit is simple," Dreissig smiled, satisfied with my answers. "I understand he will arrive about midnight. The usual arrangements to bring the gold have been made and it will arrive sometime before dawn. My men will unload it and store it away. You realize, of course, that only my most trusted men take part in our operations here at the *schloss* . . . the castle, excuse me. Then tomorrow, a bit of sport for relaxation. I understand His Excellency is bringing his two most successful birds with him."

I nodded. It seemed the right place for a wise nod.

"After dinner," Dreissig went on, "we will lay plans for our initial joint moves."

This was not the spiel I was after. I decided to toss out a line and see if he'd go for it.

"I am to take over a greater part of the operational detail." I began. "But I may not be able to take part in your discussion tomorrow night. His Excellency has asked if you would go over the broad outlines of your plan with me. He said that only you, Herr Dreissig, could impart the inspirational elements so important to understand."

I complimented myself. It sounded pretty good for someone groping in the dark. Dreissig puffed up and went for it like one of his eagles going for a chicken.

"My pleasure, Ben Kemat," he said, pointing with a long, thin finger to the map of Israel. "Here is our enemy, yours and mine, though perhaps for different reasons. Israel is the enemy of the Arab peoples today as she has been for thousands of years. The Jews want to rule and make the Arab people their servants. The Jews are not important in Germany today, but they are determined to fight us from the outside. Israel is the emotional heart of the Jews. When the heart is killed the enemy is dead."

He paused for a drink of water from a karafe on the desk.

"The Jews plot against a united Germany from outside. They plot against a united Arab front from Israel. Peace in the world can only come when the Jews give up Israel and their plots against Germany. But, and here is what His Excellency has recognized, the Jews must be forced to see the error of their ways. The Russians will never help you against the Israelis, except for some material equipment. The Russian army has never been any good outside of Russia. Its equipment is not designed to fight in the heat and the sand of the Middle East. The Americans will never help you defeat the Jews. They are filled with Jewish propaganda about morality and Judeo-Christian relations.

"What the Arab people need is a German-trained and German-staffed fighting force. Such a force of fierce Arab warriors, led by German military genius, will destroy Israel once and for all. My military advisors have already drawn up the military blueprint. We will use the technique developed by Rommel with certain added innovations. We will cut Israel into thirds and then move across and down. It will be the old *schwerpunkt und aufrollen* used simultaneously in three carefully selected spots. The name Lawrence of Arabia will be forgotten when I am finished. It will be Heinrich of Arabia the world will remember."

I almost laughed out loud. Not with that name, chum, I said to myself. With a name like that you've got two strikes against you. To Dreissig, of course, it wasn't ludicrous. To anyone else, it was downright funny, too funny to take seriously. Or was it? I seemed to remember another character with the musical comedy name of Adolf Schickelgruber who made it big. Too big. Suddenly Heinrich of Arabia didn't sound so funny any more.

Dreissig was on again and my attention snapped

back to him. His eyes were shining, his voice full of fervor. It was the same brand of twisted evangelism that blew up the world not too many years ago. It was packaged more cleverly this time, with fewer raw edges, and therefore twice as dangerous. As I listened to him I kept hearing echoes, old refrains that had been changed a little, but were still the same tune. New wine in old bottles.

"You understand," Dreissig went on, "our quarrel with the Jews is not racial at all, but a result of their political bias. It is their political stand against the Arab peoples, asserted by their military posture. It is their political stand against the reunification of Germany, asserted by their wealth and connections. That is why we will move on two fronts—politically here at home, in Germany, under my direction, and militarily against Israel. When it is over, the world will know the names of Heinrich Dreissig and Abdul Ben Mussaf."

Old wine in new bottles. I said it again to myself, because that's what it was. The arched window behind him told me that it had gotten dark outside, and I wanted to get Dreissig off his soap-box. I still had some important questions.

"A glorious vision, Herr Dreissig," I cut in. "The gold shipment tonight, it will come the usual way, you say?"

"Yes, on barges up the Rhine to my private landing here," he said.

"Very good," I smiled. It had been a most informative briefing, much more so than my neo-Nazi host had any idea. I was thinking of how to broach the last question, where was he stashing the stuff, when there were loud voices outside. Three of the guards burst in with a fourth figure, a figure in a clinging red jersey and blue-on-blue checked slacks.

I closed my eyes slowly. Oh, God, no, I groaned inwardly. Make it go away. But it didn't go away. I opened my eyes and the red jersey was still there.

"We found her prowling outside, trying to get near the gate and sneak in," one of the guards said. I was pretty sure Lisa hadn't recognized me in my costume. She hadn't even glanced at me, but was giving Dreissig a cool, hard stare.

"I lost my way and your big bully-boys grabbed me," she said icily. Dreissig smiled at her.

"She may be working with the American agent," he addressed the guards. "Take her downstairs to the torture chamber. We'll have her talking soon enough." He turned to me. "These old castles still have their uses," he said. "The old medieval torture chamber in the cellar can't be beat by anything today."

A guard started to pull Lisa away, but she shook him off and walked out on her own. I watched her go out, back straight, head high.

Lisa Huffmann, I said to myself, if they don't kill you I'm going to fan your little ass so hard you won't be able to sit for a month.

VIII

Dreissig asked me to join him for something to eat prior to the midnight repast he was setting for Ben Mussaf's arrival. All I could do was think of Lisa, with my emotions alternating between anger at her damned nosiness and concern for her life. Dreissig, for all his Nazi echoes and his musical-comedy ideas of grandeur, was playing for keeps. Beneath the smooth rhetoric, the polished propaganda, beat the soul of a dangerous dictator, I was convinced. I thought of pulling Wilhelmina out and blowing his head off right here and now, but I didn't dare. I didn't know how much he had borrowed from his veiled idol, Adolf Hitler. If his followers were imbued with the same *Götterdämmerung* philosophy, the death of their leader could touch off an orgy of self-destruction and wild killing. Lisa would be as good as dead then for sure. I wouldn't place bets on my own chances either.

No, I'd wait. Dreissig was dangerous, but I wanted to see how far Ben Mussaf went along. I had the feeling that the Arab could see only one thing through his congenital tunnel vision, a chance to get at Israel. He had, I felt sure, bought the very attractive military aspects of Dreissig's plan and not the twisted, distorted anti-Semitism that was a part of Dreissig. The Arabs were material realists. Even their hatred of Israel was subject to that realistic approach to life. Even now, certain groups were taking a realistic approach to the existence of Israel. It was the diehards like Ben Mussaf and the political activists such as Nasser who kept the pot boiling. But I was betting that if Ben Mussaf saw his new-found mentor go up in smoke, he'd pack his chips away and forget the whole idea in the light of reality. It was worth a try anyway. Besides, I had really no choice until I got Lisa Huffmann out of here.

I begged off Dreissig's dinner invitation and told him I'd like to go down to the medieval torture chamber to observe first-hand. He had one of the guards show me the way down the dark, gloomy, forbidding stone steps. I noted we passed the wine-cellar entrance and were entering a subbasement. We passed rows of old wooden boxes I recognized with a chill were ancient coffins piled up outside the chamber itself, which was lighted by kerosene torches.

"We don't use it that much," the guard explained. "Herr Dreissig saw no reason to install electricity down here. Besides, it adds to the atmosphere, doesn't it?"

"Definitely," I agreed. The sight of a man, stark naked and chained to wall irons, also added to the atmosphere.

"He tried to steal from Herr Dreissig," the guard explained. "His final punishment comes tomorrow, I understand."

The man showed signs of having been somewhat more than scolded. His chest and arms were a mass of red welts and there were burn marks on his abdomen. We had reached the main room of the chamber and an awe-inspiring collection of torture instruments lined the walls and occupied the center of the place. Along with an assortment of whips and chains, there were racks, torture wheels, places for hanging one up by any part of the anatomy, hot forges for burning and gouging and a number of delightful appliances I could only guess at.

The three guards had brought Lisa to the center of the huge room where, in flickering torchlight, one was holding her arms pinned behind her back while the other two undressed her. I arrived for the finishing touch as he pulled down her panties, black with pink trim. Lisa's eyes were filled with tears, her cheeks wet and flushed. Her breasts were, as I'd suspected, upturned and beautifully curved, pink tips thrusting out invitingly. Her legs were long, with tapered thighs and lovely calves, her body slender and curving into a smooth, flat abdomen. She had a figure for fitting in close to one's body, reveling in the excitement of bodily touch.

I stayed in the shadows, looking on as one of the guards pawed those beautiful breasts. Lisa tore an arm free and clawed at his face in tearful fury. The guard drew back, felt the blood on his cheeks, and hit her across the face with the back of his hand. She fell back against the torture wheel, the others seized her and strapped her onto the device. It was brutally simple. The victim was strapped onto the wheel by thick, leather straps that fitted around each thigh, across the abdomen and each forearm. Each turn of the wheel tightened the straps, shutting down the circulation while increasing the pain in a horrible contest between death and pain.

"Some people," the guard with me explained, "have had kidneys and other organs burst from the pressure and still lived on for an amazingly long period."

"Fascinating," I commented. They turned the wheel hard, three complete turns. I saw the leather tighten and bite down into Lisa's lovely abdomen. A long gasp of pain escaped her and I could see the wild fear in her eyes.

"Who sent you here?" the guard asked. He spun the wheel again and I watched the strap across her abdomen grow taut. "Nobody," she screamed. "Stop . . . oh, God, stop!"

He turned the wheel again in a complete circle. Lisa's lovely body arched against the straps and she screamed, an agonizing, pitiful scream that reverberated in the cavernous chamber. The guards were caught up in the psychosis of sadism now, and one spun the wheel again. Lisa's scream was a gasping, crying sound and I saw her stomach quivering in pain, contracting, drawing itself in as the muscles reacted to the pressure across her groin. She was crying steadily now, pitiful, wracking sobs. I had held back hoping they'd stop on their own and I'd get the chance to sneak back later and free her. But as I saw one of them reach to turn the wheel again, I knew that my hope was a hollow one.

A heavy iron bar rested against a rack inches from my hand. I grabbed it, bashed the nearest guard with a sweeping blow and let the momentum carry me forward to smash it against the second one. The other two whirled in surprise. I drove the iron into the first one's stomach, feeling the rip of cartilage and muscle. The second of the two was reaching into his pocket. He never made it. I tapped his jaw with the length of iron and he went down atop his friend. What the hell, I said. My cover would be shot the moment Ben Mussaf arrived anyway. I unstrapped Lisa, eased her to the ground to let her gather some strength back.

"Hold still," I said, slipping the jersey over her head. She looked up, recognition dawning in her eyes.

"Nick!" she gasped, immediately clutching the jersey to her breasts.

"Never mind the modesty," I said gruffly. "Besides, it's too late. Just get your things on." I let her dress while I tossed off the burnoose and the robe. The damned thing was a pain in the ass to me. It interfered with my freedom of action. I grabbed Lisa and headed up the stairs, detouring at the entrance to the wine cellar.

"In here," I said. It was as good a place as any to hole up. They'd be searching for us soon enough, I knew. We sat in a corner, in the deepest of the shadows, the huge wine casks looming up all around us.

"My stomach," Lisa groaned. "It'll never be the same again."

"Yes, it will," I grunted. "They were only starting on you. I stepped in, because I saw you were not up to taking any more. You know, if I get you out of this place alive, I'm coming back and kick you around Kaiserlautern Strasse. What a damn fool stunt to pull. What the hell got into you?"

"I'm sorry," she said contritely. "I've made it worse for you, haven't I? I wanted to see if I could help you. I had the feeling something dangerous was happening."

She sobbed and I put my arm around her. She snuggled up to me at once. "Can you ever forgive me?" she asked humbly.

"I may not have to," I answered. "If I can't come up with a way to get you out of here, I may have to leave you sitting right here until I can get back."

I suddenly slapped my leg in anger. We were sitting here when there was the rear entrance, the way I'd come in to the castle earlier. Lisa's hand in mine, I hurried past the wine kegs to the two oak doors. I was glad that my normal caution asserted itself and I opened the door only a crack. It was enough for me to see that the rear of the castle was lined with guards, some seated on hand dollies, others leaning on four-wheel flatbed handcarts. They were obviously marking time, waiting for something, but they effectively prevented that way out. We returned to the corner and sat down. She came up against me at once, her body soft and sweet in my arms.

My eyes wandered up and down the rows of kegs as I tried to figure another way of getting Lisa out. Suddenly it exploded in me. I knew what had been bothering me about this damned wine cellar.

"This is a phony wine cellar, Lisa," I announced calmly.

"You sure?" she asked, sitting up and peering into the darkness.

"I'd bet on it," I said. "I knew something was wrong, but I couldn't put my finger on it till just now. Look at the top of each cask, where the bung—the stopper—is. You see that every one of the bungs is at the top of the cask."

Lisa nodded. "In any wine cellar that is a real, working wine cellar," I went on, "some of the wine has been racked, which means drawn off into clean, sulphured casks. This is done three times. With the third racking, the cask is stored on its side so that the bung will be completely covered with wine. This prevents any air seeping into the cask. Not a one of these casks is racked with the bung on the side of the cask."

I moved beside the nearest row of casks. I tapped the front part, ran my fingers across the top and onto the bottom end. I heard the faint, dense sound of wine inside. I knelt down and felt along the underside of the casks. My fingers quickly found the thin ridge in the wood and I traced it around to form a square about two by two feet. I pressed up on the square of wood until it gave way at one end to hang down. Reaching up into the hole, from which no wine poured forth, my hands felt the touch of burlap covering an oblong, hard object. I had found where the gold was kept. Each cask had a false, hollowed-out underside.

I had just replaced the square of wood when we heard the sounds of voices and feet running up and down the stone steps outside. They had discovered the guards and Lisa's disappearance. The Arab's robes in a pile completed the picture for them. I'd hoped they would leave searching the wine cellar for the very end, or perhaps not at all, but as luck would have it they burst in almost at once. Flashlights probed the darkness, sweeping toward the corner where we huddled. That time was at hand, either fight or give up. As the latter one never appealed to me without trying the first, I pegged two shots at the flashlights, heard the gasps and saw the lights swing up into the air in a crazy pattern.

"Stay close to me, honey," I called to Lisa. "We're going to make a run for it."

We emerged onto the stone stairway as two more guards came rushing down. Wilhelmina barked again, twice, and they toppled down the steps. We were out on the main floor and I ducked behind a corner, pulling Lisa in with me, as a half-dozen of the white-shirted men raced by to fan out into various parts of the castle. I waited a moment, then raced out, heading for the main gate. All I wanted to do was get Lisa on her way down to the car. We never made it. A horde of them met us as they came rushing in from outside. I dropped two more and turned and ran back into the castle proper.

The walls of the main corridor were hung with various kinds of medieval battle implements. I jumped up and yanked down a vicious item called by the incongruous name of morning star. It consisted of a spiked steel ball at the end of a long chain that was attached to a pole. Lisa had flattened herself against the wall as the horde charged me. I swung the medieval weapon with all my might. The spiked steel ball whirled in an arc and I saw at least four of them go down, blood spurting from gaping wounds. I kept the spiked ball swinging as I moved forward. Three more went down. The damned thing was positively great. A pair of hands grabbed at me from behind. Other arms tackled my legs. I staggered, intent on keeping the morning star whirling. More of them were there now, but staying at a respectful distance. I flung the damned thing at them and turned my attention to the three clinging to me. I detached one with a hard right and I was working on the second one clinging to my legs when something hard exploded against the back of my head. The stone walls turned to rubber. Another blow crashed against my temple and I felt myself going down, my ribs hurting from kicks and blows. A curtain of darkness came down over me.

When I woke, the lights were bright and I heard the hum of voices all around me. My wrists seemed terribly heavy and I focused on them to see the steel shackles encircling them. Hands pulled me to my feet roughly. The haze cleared and I first saw Lisa standing beside me, also shackled. Then I saw Dreissig, still impeccably dressed, standing beside a shorter man, expensively robed. Ben Mussaf had arrived and his entourage of aides was standing behind him. Dreissig was pridefully explaining how they had seized us. I noticed an Arab next to Ben Mussaf holding two cages, each containing a hooded falcon.

"They will make an excellent test for us tomorrow, no, Your Excellency?" Dreissig addressed the Arab. Ben Mussaf nodded, his face without change of expression, his eyes as sharp and piercing as those of his falcon. I had the distinct impression that Ben Mussaf was not at all happy at finding Dreissig's hideaway had been penetrated by outsiders.

"These are the only two?" he asked, glancing sharply up at Dreissig.

"We've searched the grounds thoroughly," Dreissig answered. "The American has been a thorn in our side for days. He is a famous agent of their organization AXE."

Ben Mussaf grunted and Dreissig ordered the guards to take us downstairs. As we were pulled away, I heard Ben Mussaf tell Dreissig that his men would be with the gold on the barges until it was safely unloaded. Lisa and I were shackled to wall irons in the torture chamber and left. I glanced over at her.

"You know what I think?" I asked her. "I think Aunt Anna isn't going shopping today."

She bit her lip and her eyes were dark with concern.

"What are they going to do with us?" she asked.

"I don't know," I answered honestly. "Whatever it is, you can be sure you won't like it. Get some sleep."

"Sleep?" she cried out, incredulous. "You're joking. How could you?"

"Easy. Just watch." I closed my eyes, put my head back against the wall and was asleep in moments. I'd learned, years ago, in many kinds of places and situations, that there was a time for sleeping and a time for fighting. They were equally important and I'd learned to make the best of both.

I woke with the dawn and smiled. Lisa was still

asleep alongside me. As I'd expected, exhaustion had taken over eventually. The morning wore on and no one came down. It was nearly midday when Lisa awoke. The other prisoner, still stark naked, lay chained across the room, stirring occasionally, but otherwise silent and unmoving. Except for a quiet good morning, Lisa was silent and her eyes showed her fear. She would glance at me, trying to muster her cool, contained composure, but it wasn't successful.

Midday passed on into the afternoon and still we were left alone. I was beginning to hope that perhaps something had gone wrong when I heard the white-shirted guards approaching. They unshackled Lisa first, then me and then the small naked man across the room. We were marched up the stairs and out into the late afternoon sun. A half-dozen additional men joined us as we were marched up into the hills and through a woodland path to emerge on a broad, gently sloping expanse of beautifully trimmed lawn. I saw the cluster of figures at the top of the slope. Dreissig was there, wearing riding britches, and Ben Mussaf in his robes. Three Arabs stood behind them, each one holding a golden eagle on his wrist. I was getting very uneasy. I knew damned well they hadn't brought us out here for a friendly exhibition of bird watching and I was so right.

"Sorry we had to keep you waiting," Dreissig said with sadistic unctuousness to his smile. "But His Excellency and I changed our schedule and had our planning session during the day instead of at night."

"I thought maybe you were busy counting your gold," I answered blandly. Dreissig smiled the charmingly evil smile again.

"No, that will be done tonight, I'm afraid," he said. "The barges did not arrive till nearly dawn and as the unloading process is a lengthy one we decided to wait till night and make certain we were not observed by river traffic."

"I fear you will not be around, either, to observe," Ben Mussaf said, extending an arm to let the handler transfer one of the eagles to his wrist. "These magnificent hunters are the latest and most successful in an interesting experiment. They have been especially trained to hunt not birds, but man. I introduced Herr Dreissig to the sport of falconry and he interested me in this variation, golden eagles as natural dive bombers, capable of picking out and destroying a courier or fleeing prisoner with ease. It's a fantastic innovation. The golden eagle, as you know, is a born hunter and killer. He will often attack anything that moves so it was not a question of developing an instinct, but specializing it."

"As we are sportsmen," Dreissig cut in, "we are giving each of you a sporting chance at your freedom." He pointed to a thicket of woods at the bottom of the green slope, some 500 yards away. "If you can reach those trees alive," he said, "you will be allowed your freedom."

I smiled wryly. Having seen both falcons and eagles in action, I knew what kind of odds he was giving us. Ben Mussaf raised his arm, the hooded eagle moved, sensing the moment that was about to approach. The little man, still stark naked, was shoved out in front. I saw Lisa's eyes fill with pity and concern.

"Go, pig!" Dreissig yelled, giving the small nude figure a shove. The man glanced back, his eyes suddenly coming alive, and he began to run with a desperate speed.

"Unstrike the hood!" Ben Mussaf ordered the handler who immediately pulled the drawstrings open at the back of the eagle's hood. With a flick of his hand, Ben Mussaf snatched the hood from the eagle, lifted his arm and the eagle soared into the air. I watched the eagle wheel slowly in the air, executing a wide circle, and then start its swooping dive. The little man was halfway down the hill and I felt Lisa's hand pressing into my arm. "He's going to make it!" she whispered excitedly. I didn't say anything. The horrible truth would be spread out there before her eyes in seconds. I watched the eagle hurtling down with bullet-like speed. As the great golden wings neared the man, they spread out flat and leveled off to brake and come down with talons extended. I saw the vicious talons swipe across the man's head, saw the gusher of blood that erupted. We could hear his scream of pain easily, as he clutched both hands to his head, stumbled, fell and rolled over. He got up and started running again, but the eagle had turned at the end of its swoop and came soaring past to strike again, talons ripping deep into his arms. As the great bird rose up into the air, it pulled one of his arms up, half-lifting the man from the ground. This time the eagle dived directly without executing its long swoop. Once again the vicious talons sunk into face and neck, ripping and tearing. Shrieking in agony, the little man dropped to the ground. The eagle came down again, a whirling mass of wings and feathers, striking deeply now with its hooked beak, tearing at the flesh of the man's stomach. It was a sickening sight as the great hawk, in a frenzy of killing, continued to strike at the naked body until it was a lifeless mass of torn and shredded flesh. Finally, Ben Mussaf blew a high-pitched, shrill whistle, the eagle paused, looked up and finally returned, landing on his wrist with bloodied talons and beak. I looked at Lisa. She had buried her face in her hands. The handler hooded the eagle at once and went off back to the castle.

"A marvelous exhibition," Dreissig said admiringly. "The girl is next. Take her clothes off." Lisa stood still for the indignity with resignation. I knew what would happen. She would have no more chance than the little man had. That lovely body would be nothing more than a blood-streaked, torn carcass in minutes from now. The only thing that could prevent it was to do away with the eagles and I had no chance of doing that. But as the thought flashed through my mind, I realized that while I couldn't do away with them, they could do away with each other. They were kept hooded till the moment of release because they would tear each other to bits at the first chance. Lisa was naked now, and Dreissig, Ben Mussaf and everyone else were busy taking in her loveliness.

"It seems a pity," the Arab suggested.

"Yes, but she will pay for the death of our Helga," Dreissig said. "An eye for an eye, your Excellency."

No one was watching me and I'd moved backwards behind the handlers holding the two eagles. I watched Dreissig grab Lisa and send her stumbling forward. "Run," he shouted. "Run, you little bitch." Lisa took off, her lovely, lithe figure a gorgeous wraith racing across the grass. Ben Mussaf reached back to receive the second of the eagles when I whisked the hoods from both eagles with one motion and gave a yell. With a flapping of wings, both birds shot into the air, circled in their wide arc and went at each other. They collided in mid-air with a shower of feathers and blood. Separating for an instant, they attacked again, talons and beaks clawing and tearing at each other in fury. They rose and fell together, swooped apart for an instant and returned to the attack. Blood flew through the air. It was deadly savagery, almost too fast for the eye to follow. Suddenly, in mid air, there was a particularly violent shudder and it was over. They plummeted to the ground, victor hardly more alive than vanquished. Dreissig and Ben Mussaf had been as transfixed by the spectacle as I was, but now their eyes turned to me in fury. I glanced beyond them. Lisa was out of sight in the woods.

"Go after her," Dreissig ordered six of his men. "Bring her back."

"You promised her freedom if she could reach the woods," I protested. "You haven't any morality, have you?"

Dreissig, his handsome face now contorted in fury, slapped me across the face. It was open handed, but it made my head snap. He was a strong sonofabitch. If he expected me to react with respectful fear he made a mistake. I let him have one right in the pit of his stomach. He doubled over, clutching his hands to his midsection and dropped to his knees. Four guards grabbed me before I had a chance to give him another one in the head.

"Take him away," Ben Mussaf ordered the guards as he helped Dreissig to his feet. I went with them quietly. They took me back to the dungeon and snapped the wrist locks on me again. It was dark within an hour and I was still alone. As time went on I began to grow optimistic. They hadn't found Lisa. Maybe she got away. I wouldn't permit myself the luxury of optimism until the night wore on, but finally I began to relax. Now all I had to do was worry about getting myself out of here, getting to Dreissig and doing a wrecking job on his schemes. That was all . . . only that wasn't all.

IX

I had been listening for the sounds of Dreissig's men moving the gold shipment into the wine cellar. They'd be using the rear entranceway, but the cellar wasn't that far from the torture chamber. I would be able to hear. But they hadn't started yet, apparently. At least my straining ears hadn't picked up anything. It was as silent as death in the cavernous room, and I immediately tensed as my ears picked up the faint sounds of footsteps creeping toward me. I peered through the dim flicker of the torchlight and suddenly saw the flash of red.

"Not again!" I exclaimed. "What the hell are you doing back here?"

"I couldn't make it out by myself," Lisa said. "They had the outer grounds tightly sealed with patrols so I came back here for your help. You got me into this, now you can get me out."

"Like hell I did," I protested. "You came snooping around after me and got yourself into it."

She smiled. "A minor technical point," she said. She reached up and unlatched the wrist irons. The fear and resignation had gone and her eyes were cool and assured once again. I remarked on the change.

"I was afraid and hurt and feeling guilty, I guess," she said. "Now I'm just mad."

"Where'd you get your clothes?"

"Where they left them on the grass," she answered. "When I saw I wasn't going to make it past the guards, I hid in the woods, nearly froze to death, and then went back up the lawn and found my clothes. I only slipped on my blouse and slacks."

She needn't have told me. I had already noticed the outline of her lovely breasts pressed against the clinging material, the small, pointed tips clearly delineated. They were two of the best reasons I knew for getting us both out of there alive and in one piece.

"I passed the landing," she said as I stood up. "They haven't started to transfer the gold yet. Ben Mussaf's men are still guarding the barges."

"How many?" I asked. "Or didn't you notice a little item like that?"

"I counted six," she snapped out, "three on each barge."

"Good girl," I said. "We'll make a spy out of you yet."

"Do you know that I still don't know what this is all about?" she said, following me up the stairs. "Except for what I've picked up, you haven't explained anything to me."

"I'll give you the whole picture when we get out of here," I said. "That's a promise. And if we don't get out, you won't need to wonder about it."

The bit with the eagles had triggered my mind into using Dreissig's own tricks against him. So the barges full of gold were still at the landing; I was sure that the gold was disguised as something else, masquerading as some other kind of shipment. A thought was rapidly forming in my mind, one that would not only hurt the bastards, but make recovery an impossibility. I paused as we reached the main hallway and removed another piece of ancient weaponry from the wall, this time taking down a heavy, sharp-bladed battle-ax. I needed something quiet and efficient, and the battle-ax would do perfectly. Since my experience with the efficiency of the morning star, I was developing a respect and a fondness for these medieval weapons. We crept to the front gate this time, as I remembered that the rear doors to the wine cellar had been blocked off by guards preparing to move the gold. They were no doubt still there. Only one white-shirted guard stood at the main gate. I crept up and tapped him gently with the flat of the battle-ax. We dumped him into the dry ditch of the moat, after I appropriated a handsome dagger from his belt.

As we hurried down toward the landing, I realized that Dreissig's force had been reduced by a sizable number through my own efforts. I always took pride in a job well done. He had fewer men, and he had obviously decided to position most of them at the outer edges of the grounds to prevent Lisa's slipping through. I still moved cautiously though. I could smell success within reach and I didn't want it to go sour now. The barges were tied end to end to the flat landing dock. I could see four of the Arabs pacing the barges. The other two were probably lying down somewhere on the boats.

"On your stomach," I said to Lisa. "We've got to get as close as we can before moving in." It was a dark night, for which I was grateful. With Lisa beside me, we crawled forward, inching along slowly to avoid making any noise. When we were a few feet from the landing, I handed her the battle-ax.

"You take this and cut the lines tying the barges to the dock. Don't pay any attention to what I'm doing. You just cut those hawsers and set the barges free."

I waited till the nearest Arab turned his back and began his patrol toward the stern of the barge. I made it in one leap, landing silently on the balls of my feet. The dagger I'd taken from the guard was in my hand when I hit the deck of the barge. I took the first Arab swiftly and quietly, lowering him to the deck. The second one had just turned and seen me when the blade flew through the air to land in his chest. He staggered, trying to pull the metal out of his chest with both hands. I was beside him before he dropped and eased him to the deck as I retrieved the dagger. The third one was, as I'd figured, fast asleep on the transom of the barge. I made sure he stayed asleep.

I heard the thump of the battle-ax cutting into the taut hawser, felt the barge move as the rope parted. The three Arabs on the next barge had heard it, too, and had whirled. I flipped the dagger again . . . a long throw, and though I wasn't that used to the knife, I gave it everything I had. Once more it struck deeply and accurately. I saw the Arab pitch forward. The other two men were leaping off the barge and starting to race up the hill toward the castle. I made no move to stop them; I jumped off the barge as the second hawser parted and she immediately began to swing out from the landing. Lisa had cut through the first hawser holding the second barge when I took the battle-ax from her and parted the remaining hawser with one angry swing.

"Show-off," she commented. I grinned and we watched the second barge move off to join the first one as it sailed slowly down the river.

"What happens to them?" Lisa asked.

"They're carried downriver by the current and sooner or later they smash into something, a point of land, another dock, a ship, perhaps. But you can be assured that some good *burgher* will call the river police. When they examine the cargo and find what it really is, they'll have a helluva lot of gold on their hands, maybe a million dollars' worth. Neither Dreissig nor Ben Mussaf can claim it. They'd have an awful lot of embarrassing questions to answer, including smuggling."

Lisa giggled. "Neat," she said.

"Let's get back to the castle," I said. "I've unfinished business."

I only found out later, but things were already jumping at the *schloss*. The two Arab barge guards had run to Ben Mussaf with their tale of what had happened. Ben Mussaf had sailed into Dreissig.

"You bumbler," he'd screamed at the Great Man. "You utter incompetent. I bring you over a million in gold and you throw it away. How could you permit this to happen? Two agents, a man and a girl, and they disrupt your entire operation."

"The man is a very dangerous agent," Dreissig defended himself.

"He is still only one man," Ben Mussaf thundered. "You are going to lead a campaign against the Israelis? You are going to unify the Arab world behind us? You are going to go down in history as a political and military genius? I don't think so after this. If you can't run this part of your operation any better than this, you aren't the one to lead the Arab world to victory over the Jews."

"You cannot talk to me that way," Dreissig shouted.

"I am withdrawing my part in this whole venture," Ben Mussaf said. "I have no further confidence in your abilities."

"You are not backing out now," Dreissig menaced. "You have plenty more gold."

"And I shall save it for someone more efficient," the Arab answered. Dreissig pushed past Ben Mussaf and called for his guards.

"Arrest him," he said, pointing at Ben Mussaf. "Take him into the tower and keep him locked up there until I give you further orders."

"You are a madman," the Arab cried out as the guards seized him.

"And you are a hostage—my hostage," Dreissig said. "I will hold you as hostage until I receive all the gold I need. You have sons in your country. They will pay. So will your people. Take him away."

When Lisa and I reached the castle, we scrambled into the darkness of the dry moat and found a doorway into the cellar. News of what had happened had already spread like wildfire. The guards spoke openly and excitedly of it and as Lisa and I hid behind a balustrade we heard the news.

"Trouble in the Garden of Eden," I commented. Lisa suppressed a laugh and we slipped out from behind our hiding place and hurried down a corridor. I wanted to get at Dreissig, but I wanted Lisa tucked safely away in some room first. It didn't quite work out that way because of a rat, a real, four-legged rat. He was big and gray and mean looking, and he suddenly ran right across in front of us. Lisa reacted in the way most girls react to rats. She screamed and realized instantly what she had done. She had done it, all right. It was a sharp, clear scream that echoed through the whole castle. I heard the thunder of footsteps on the way. We couldn't both let ourselves be nabbed again. I dived out the nearest window, caught myself on the ledge and hung there by my fingertips. I could hear them pull Lisa off. I waited as long as my fingertips held out, then pulled myself up and back into the corridor.

I was out after Dreissig, I'd decided once and for all. The man's seizure of Ben Mussaf, after killing the two Arabs, was the convincer. He was not only dangerous, but increasingly unstable. I'd get to Lisa afterwards. As it turned out, I got to her at the same time. I headed for Dreissig's office and was nearly at the closed door when I heard Lisa scream. I hit it on the run and the door flew open to reveal Dreissig pressing the girl down on the couch. He had torn her clothes off and he had her helplessly under him, her hands both held by his own large muscular fingers. As I burst in, he rose up, spun Lisa around in front of him and held her there in shield-like fashion.

He circled behind his desk, picked up a letter opener and moved out to the center of the room. I was expecting his next move and was prepared for it. With a sudden motion, he flung Lisa at me, expecting I'd automatically move to catch her and be off balance. Instead, I side-stepped, caught Lisa by one arm and using the principles of centrifugal force, sent her sailing back onto the couch. Dreissig's lunge with the letter opener found me in position. I ducked under it, caught his arm and twisted. He screamed and dropped the weapon as he sailed into the wall. As he bounced off the wall I caught him with a hard right. It sent him crashing out into the hallway. I was after him at once, but he scrambled to his feet and backed toward one wall where a collection of long polearms was mounted. I saw what he was about to do and dove at him, catching him around the knees. He brought both hands down hard on the back of my head, and I saw skyrockets. He kicked himself loose as I fell face forward on the stones, and I heard the sound of his taking down one of the long polearms. I did a quick roll as he brought the blade of the long halberd crashing down on the stones. I scrambled to my feet and ducked another vicious slash of the halberd. He had the long pole thrust under one arm now and he waited for his chance to drive it into me. I moved back against the stone wall and let him think he had me in position. He lunged and I twisted my body around as the halberd tore at my shirt. This time I grabbed the long pole as it bounced from the stones, twisted and tore it out of Dreissig's grasp. It was too unwieldy to swing around. I let it drop and went after him.

His lips were tight and snarling as he drove a hard right at me. I parried it, tried a left and found he could box. But the last thing I wanted was a time-consuming boxing contest. I was surprised some of his boys hadn't shown up already. I weaved and came up under his guard with a sharp left to the point of the rib cage. I saw him wince and dip his left side. I grabbed his left arm, avoiding a vicious right, and using close-combat techniques, sent him crashing to the floor. He lay there, unmoving. I went over and moved his head from side to side. There was nothing broken, but he was out cold. I looked up to see Lisa at the doorway. She had thrown her clothes on. As I looked at her, I saw her eyes widen, saw the warning form on her lips. I knew there was no room to turn around. I dropped forward in a crouch as Dreissig's blow whistled over my head. As it was, the momentum carried him into me and I fell forward, twisting as I did so to land on my back. Dreissig, I saw, was very much conscious. The bastard had played possum on me. He dived at me and I met him with a sharp kick. I felt the crunch of his chest bone as my foot landed and he fell backwards. I was on my feet and after him, and this time there'd be no more tricks. I caught him with a right that spun him around. He tried to cover up, but a left straightened him out and another right landed flush on his jaw. I felt the jawbone crack. He fell back heavily and lay there, his face twisted in pain, small bubbles forming on his lips. I reached down and picked him up by the shirt. The long pole came up with his body and I saw what had happened. He had fallen onto the sharp edge of the halberd. The blade had gone half through his body between his shoulder blades. Heinrich Dreissig was dead. The phoenix of Naziism had died with him.

I was still thinking about why none of Dreissig's guards had shown up to help him when I smelled the acrid odor of fire. I looked at Lisa. Her eyes were wide. Down the corridor, black smoke was beginning to billow up from below. I ran to the top of the stone stairs and saw the flames raging below on the main floor. Old tables, chairs and other furniture had been piled up to get the fire going. The dry tapestries and banners on the walls were beginning to catch fire. The construction of the old castle would create a terrific updraft in no time at all. The heat and smoke would rush up into every corner and crevice. Now I understood why none of his boys had shown. He'd instructed them all to set the place on fire.

I'd been right in my original fears about him emulating his idol with the *Götterdämmerung* bit. I'd put it aside and forgotten about it, unfortunately. Yet even now it didn't seem quite right. He had decided to hold Ben Mussaf as a hostage for continued gold shipments. Why throw it all away in a blaze of glory? I went back to Lisa.

"Did Dreissig say anything to you when he brought you up here?" I asked. "Anything that might be important?"

"He said he was going to rape me before getting out of here," she answered.

"Before getting out of here," I repeated. "That doesn't sound like he intended to go up in flames himself. Was there anything else?"

"Well, when he was . . . when he was . . ."

"Knock off the modesty routine," I yelled at her.

"When he was on top of me," she blurted out, "he said he'd like to take me with him, but I'd be in the way. He said he'd have enough trouble with the Arab and his pets."

It was beginning to make more sense now. Dreissig figured the whole routine here had been overexposed. Too many mistakes, too many of his bully-boys in on it, too many possibilities of being in danger from Ben Mussaf's faithful. He was going to shoot the whole works up and let it appear that he'd gone up with it. But actually, he was planning to get out with Ben Mussaf as hostage and start operations from someplace else. I heard Lisa cough, and felt the sharp stinging in my lungs, too. The castle was rapidly filling up with the deadly smoke and fumes. The lung-searing blasts of heat would be coming up soon. If Dreissig was planning a getaway he had to have some way already figured out.

"Stay here, keep the door closed," I told Lisa. "I'm going to get Ben Mussaf."

I tied a handkerchief around my face and made my way through the smoke to the stairs. It was very heavy there and I felt my lungs swelling. The heat was almost intolerable as I climbed up the steps. It hadn't reached up to the tower as thickly yet, but it was simply a matter of time. I found the door to the cell and peered through the slotted opening. Ben Mussaf was inside, looking very worried. I slid the bolt open and he rushed out.

"Dreissig's dead, and this place is about to become a gigantic oven," I told him. "Unless I can find a way out, we're going to be well done. Follow me."

Ben Mussaf nodded and his eyes were a mixture of gratitude and apprehension. In only a few moments the smoke had grown still denser and the heat had gone up in intensity. I fought my way back down the stairs, groping along the corridor, back to the room where Lisa waited. She had kept the door closed and inside the smoke, while curling around the edges, was not yet intolerable. We could breathe and talk at least. But every moment was bringing a horrible death closer.

"Dreissig intended to get out," I said. "There must be a secret passageway someplace."

"It could be any place!" Lisa exclaimed. "To search for it in this smoke is impossible. Besides, how would we even know where to begin to look?"

"You're right, it could be any place, but I don't think it is," I said between coughs. "You said he intended to take Ben Mussaf and his pets. That means he was probably going to pick them up on the way. Come on . . . we've one chance and nothing to lose by taking it."

I led the way, dropping to my knees to crawl along the floor. It wasn't a great improvement, but it did make a difference as the smoke sought to rise upwards at all times. But the stones were getting blisteringly hot. I figured we had maybe two or three minutes to find a way out of this place or else. I managed to feel my way to the first room where most of the eagles were kept and I was encouraged to see the door tightly shut. We opened it and fell gasping into the still relatively breathable air inside the closed room. The side walls were obstructed by old cages and crates and training equipment, but the wall at the far end was clear. A series of wooden panels designed beneath a mantle adorned the smooth surface. I gestured to it. "Start pressing everything you can," I ordered.

Ben Mussaf and Lisa followed me in pushing and pressing against the wall. Suddenly, as Lisa pressed upon a panel in the lower corner, the wall moved and swung open. I led the way down the narrow passageway. Even in the winding, steep tunnel, the walls were hot. The passageway was half-ramp and half-steps, winding and twisting. Finally I saw a narrow doorway ahead. I felt it first, laying my hands upon it to test its temperature. For all I knew the passageway could open out into a wildly blazing room. Dreissig would have been out long before this, I reminded everyone. But the door was relatively cool. I pushed and stumbled out into what seemed to be a woodshed. Another door beckoned, and I pushed it open to feel the cool fresh air of the night. We stepped out, and I saw that the passageway had led us underground and out to the little woodshed a hundred yards or so from the castle.

I felt Lisa's hand creep into mine as we turned to look up at the great castle. It was ablaze with tongues of flame leaping out of the center, running along the battlements and flickering out of windows. It looked as though a medieval army had lain siege to it and, in a way, there was truth to it. An army of medieval ideas had lain siege to it, discredited ideas about superior peoples and racial myths, about inherited guilt and collective enmities.

"Where did you park the car?" I asked Lisa, and laughed as I heard myself. It sounded as though we'd just come out of a neighborhood movie.

"Down the road," she said. "Come on, I'll show you."

I turned to Ben Mussaf. The Arab's fierce eyes were piercing but uncertain.

"I owe you my life," he said. "I am eternally grateful. I realize I am your prisoner, of course."

I'd been waiting for this moment to come up and I'd given it some fleeting thought. There were no real technical grounds on which to hold Ben Mussaf, though I was certain I could come up with something based on conspiracy, perhaps even accessory to murder. But that really wasn't important any longer. I'd made up my mind to let him go. It would show the West's magnanimity and willingness to forgive and forget. Mostly, though, it would be a lesson he would not soon forget.

"You are free to go," I told him. I saw his eyes deepen in surprise. "I suggest you pick your friends more carefully and for better reasons. You've been running around in the wrong company. There are some nice Jewish boys who live near you. Why don't you go play with them and become good neighbors?"

Ben Mussaf said nothing, but he got the message. He bowed, turned on his heel and walked away. I took Lisa's hand and we headed for the car. Dreissig's boys had all scattered to the winds by now. They were not worth trying to collect. Their kind would always be around, the alienated, willing to serve any master.

X

When we arrived at Lisa's temporary residence there was a note from her aunt on the table.

"Dear Lisa,

Frau Schutzen invited me to spend a few days in the country with her. When you did not return last night, I decided to go. I'll be back Friday afternoon, late.

Aunt Anna

"Do you have some place to stay?" Lisa asked shyly, giving me a sideways glance.

"Yes," I said. "Right here."

Her head went up and the cool, bemused expression surveyed me. "I have my misgivings about this," she said.

"Don't worry," I grinned down at her. "You'll be as safe as you want to be."

She thought that over and then accepted it.

"I'm going to shower and clean up," she said. "I feel like a smoked ham."

"I'm next in line. While you're showering I'm going to call my boss in the States. Collect . . . don't get excited."

I watched her go into the bedroom, her breasts moving deliciously under the red jersey, unconfined by a brassiere. I sat down and put in a call to Hawk. I couldn't get through until after I'd showered and freshened up. Lisa had made the bed for me and fixed the couch for herself. We were arguing about who would take the couch when the phone jangled. It was the overseas operator with my call.

"The Arabs were financing Dreissig," I informed him. "In particular one Abdul Ben Mussaf."

"Were?" Hawk's flat voice came over. For someone who made it a policy to speak in a monotone he could put a lot of inflection in just one word.

"Were," I repeated. "Dreissig's dead and Ben Mussaf has picked up his marbles and gone home. Oh, one more thing," I said. "West Germany is going to be richer by about a million dollars in gold bars found on two barges on the Rhine."

"Good work, N3," Hawk said. "You've outdone yourself on this. You deserve a rest. Take tomorrow off. You can come back the next day."

"*Tomorrow?*" I exclaimed. "Don't spoil me. Three or four hours is more than enough."

Hawk's silence was voluble. "All right," he said.

"When do you want to come back? When will you have enough of her?"

"This weekend and never, in that order," I said.

"All right, but be sure you're here Saturday. Or at your place, at least. I may have something important by then."

He clicked off and I turned to Lisa. "I have until Saturday. That's when I head back for the States," I announced.

"You head out of here Friday night," she said. "Before Aunt Anna comes back."

Lisa had a light blue lounging robe on, and from the way it fell, nothing else. With most girls, I'd have been able to get a lead by now. Lisa was impossible to figure. She was more than lovely, more than desirable. She was truly likable and her coming after me, though a misguided move, had been touching. I didn't want to ruin what was a damn nice relationship in an off-beat sort of way. I decided to be good and not run the risk of hurting her.

"You take the bed and I'll take the couch and no more arguing about it," I said. She got up and went to the bedroom. At the door, she paused and the robe fell open enough for me to see one long, lovely leg. I remembered the young-deer beauty of her as she ran across that grass—beauty in a moment of horror. "Good night, Nick," she said.

"Sleep tight, sweetie," I answered. She flicked the light off and the room was plunged into near darkness. Reflected light from the corner street lamp outlined the furniture in the room. I had closed my eyes and stretched out when I heard the door open and she was kneeling beside me. Even in the near darkness I could see she was serious, unsmiling.

"Who are you, Nick?" she asked quietly. "You've never really told me."

I reached out and pulled her closer. "I'm someone who'd like to kiss you," I said. "Who are you?"

"I'm someone who'd like you to kiss her," she said. Her arms were around my neck, and the robe parted. My hands found her breasts, upturned, young and eager. The pink tips rose up at once as my fingers caressed them and her lips were the same honey-sweetness I'd tasted before. Only now they were eager, yearning, pressing down on mine. Her shoulders were bare as the robe dropped off entirely and she pressed her breasts against me, still on her knees alongside the couch. I pulled her up and laid her long, lithe figure against me, fitting it into the hollows and curves of my body. She was hesitant at her lovemaking at first, but as I explored her body, her lovely, long legs parted and she turned to me for more. Her own hands began to caress, and her breasts thrust themselves up for my touch.

"Oh, Nick, Nick," she murmured. "Don't ever stop . . . not tonight, not tomorrow . . . not until you have to go."

I made love to her and she responded with the wonderful, willing, tender eagerness of the young. The second time she was equally willing, equally tender and wonderful. She had found a new freedom in herself and her caresses were lovely interludes of pleasure. We did get up to eat, but for the most part we stayed together in bed for the two-and-a-half days that were ours alone. Lisa's cool, delightful sense of humor was a wonderful added spice to our lovemaking. There was a sophistication about her that was unusual in a European girl, that assured independence that usually marked the American girl. But in bed, she was all tenderness, all willing desires, all pulsating hips and quivering pelvis.

Friday afternoon came much too soon. I dressed and made sure I'd be gone before Aunt Anna returned. I was really sorry I had to leave her. It was fun to make love with a girl you could enjoy as a person as well as a bedmate.

"What plane are you taking tomorrow?" she asked at the door. I'd phoned reservations during one of the breaks in lovemaking. "The ten o'clock flight from Tempelhof," I said.

"I'll be there," she answered.

"You don't have to," I told her.

"Yes I do," she said, her eyes dancing.

I left, got a hotel room for the night and wished I could find a way to see Lisa again. I was up early and at the airport in plenty of time. It was crowded and it was getting dangerously near plane time when I saw her figure moving through the crowds toward me. She wore a lovely turquoise suit and had that air of insouciance about her.

"What happened?" I asked a little gruffly. "It's time for me to board."

"Unavoidable delays," she said, falling in step beside me. I handed my ticket to the purser and watched with a frown as she gave him a ticket.

"What are you doing?" I asked.

"Going home," she said, taking my arm and heading for the plane. I halted.

"Going home where?" I said, beginning to have a very strange feeling.

"To Milwaukee," she said coolly. "Come on, you're blocking the way."

I followed her lithe, long shape up the ramp to the plane and inside. She sat down and patted the seat next to her.

"Wait a minute," I said. "What do you mean, 'Milwaukee'? You told me you were a German girl."

"I never said anything of the kind," she answered, her eyes disdainfully hurt that I should accuse her of such a thing. Thinking back, I couldn't remember that she ever had said so in so many words.

"I'm of German descent," she said. "And I was here visiting my aunt. You just assumed I'd come from Hamburg or Düsseldorf or some such city."

"I asked you where you learned so many American expressions," I said.

"And I told you. I see a lot of American movies."

"In Milwaukee."

"In Milwaukee."

"You said you learned your English in school."

"Absolutely correct," she said, flashing me a saucy, self-satisfied grin.

I sat down. "If there weren't so many people on this plane, I'd turn you over my knee," I told her.

"You can do it when we get to New York," she said, eyes dancing again. "I promise to cooperate. You can turn me any way you like."

I found myself grinning with her again. It was going to be a great flight back. The weekend suddenly looked pretty damn good, too.

THE END

Nick Carter

The Devil's Cockpit	17½p
The Chinese Paymaster	17½p
A Korean Tiger	17½p
Seven Against Greece	17½p
Assignment Israel	17½p
Red Guard	17½p
The Filthy Five	17½p
The Bright Blue Death	17½p
Spy Castle	17½p
Macao	17½p
Operation Moon Rocket	17½p
Dragon Flame	17½p
Hanoi	17½p
Operation Starvation	17½p
The Mind Poisoners	17½p
Double Identity	17½p
Mission to Venice	20p
The China Doll	17½p
Danger Key	17½p
Checkmate in Rio	17½p
Amsterdam	17½p
Temple of Fear	17½p
Istanbul	17½p
Rhodesia	17½p
14 Seconds to Hell	17½p
The Defector	20p
Carnival for Killing	20p
The Red Rays	20p
Peking—The Tulip Affair	20p
The Amazon	20p
The Sea Trap	20p
Berlin	20p
Saigon	20p
Safari for Spies	20p
The 13th Spy	20p
A Bullet for Fidel	20p
Fraulein Spy	20p
Run Spy Run	20p
Operation Che Guevara	25p
The Doomsday Formula	25p
Operation Snake	25p
The Casbah Killers	25p
The Slavemaster	25p
The Red Rebellion	25p
The Executioners	25p
The Mind Killers	25p

War

The War Dispatches Sir Philip Gibbs 25p

Four-and-a-half years of front-line reporting from the carnage of the First World War

The Conspirators James Graham Murray 25p

These spies played for the highest stakes—and lost

RAF Biggin Hill Graham Wallace (illus.) 30p

The immortal story of one of the Battle of Britain's most famous fighter stations

The Battle of Britain (illus.) 25p

Official records from the British and German sides and the recollections of the pilots themselves. The really authentic story

Operation Cicero L. C. Moyzisch 25p

The most sensational true spy story to come out of the Second World War

Wingless Victory Sybil Hepburn 25p

An Englishwoman, trapped in Occupied France, waged a cloak-and-dagger war against the German invaders

The Valley of the Shadow H. Oloff de Wet.. .. .. 25p

Six years a prisoner of Nazi Germany, four years under sentence of death—*he survived*

Readiness at Dawn Wing-Commander Ronald Adam, O.B.E. 25p

'Thrilling action, both aloft and on the ground, vigorously portrayed'—*Illustrated London News*

We Rendezvous at Ten Wing-Commander Ronald Adam, O.B.E. 25p

'An absorbing war book, one of the finest'—*Observer*

Name ....

Address ....

Titles required...................................

....

- -